I went into a bar.

"Gimme a drink," I said to the bartender.

"Brother, don't take that drink," said a voice at my elbow. I turned and there was a skinny little guy in his fifties. Thin, yellow hair and a smile on his face. "Brother, don't take that drink," he said.

I shook him off.

"Where'd you come from?" I said. "You weren't there when I sat down here one second ago." He just grinned at me.

"Gimme a drink," I said to the bartender.

"Not for you," said the bartender. "You had enough before you came in here." A fat bartender polishing shot glasses with his little finger inside a dishtowel. "Get your friend to take you home."

"He's no friend of mine," I said.

"Brother," said the little man, "come with me."

"I want a drink," I said. An idea struck me. I turned to the little man. "Let's you and I go someplace else and have a drink," I said.

We went out of the bar together, and suddenly we were somewhere else.

GORDON R. DICKSON

GUIDED TOUR

A TOM DOHERTY ASSOCIATES BOOK

GUIDED TOUR

Copyright © 1988 by Gordon R. Dickson

First printing: February 1988

A TOR Book

Published by Tom Doherty Associates, Inc.
49 West 24 Street
New York, N.Y. 10010

ISBN: 0-812-53589-8
CAN. ED.: 0-812-53590-1

Printed in the United States of America

0 9 8 7 6 5 4 3 2 1

Acknowledgments

Contents

Guided Tour

Please keep close—
We enter by this new pale arch of hours
Into the greystone corridor of years,
Which at this end is still under construction.
Please note the stained glass windows which depict
A number of historic episodes.
A legal green here—further back they're purple—
Before that, bright iron, bronze, and last—grey flint,
From which the hall derives its general tone.
One legend goes that at the furthest part,
Where it begins, there're only two small stones
Placed one on top the other for a start
By some half-animal—but others think
The whole was laid out from the very first
By some big architect whose spirit still
Directs construction. Well, you take your pick.
. . . And now, I thought I heard somebody ask
About our future thoughts for building on.
Well, there's now building quite a fine addition
Of plastic, steel and glass, all air-conditioned,
Also there's planned a nucleonic part
Built up from force-fields. But beyond *its* end
We butt, unfortunately, on a space—
A pit, or void, through which the right of way
May be disputed, and is still in doubt. . . .

The Monkey Wrench

Cary Harmon was not an ungifted young man. He had the intelligence to carve himself a position as a Lowland society lawyer, which on Venus is not easy to do. And he had the discernment to consolidate that position by marrying into the family of one of the leading drug-exporters. But, nevertheless, from the scientific viewpoint, he was a layman; and laymen, in their ignorance, should never be allowed to play with delicate technical equipment; for the result will be trouble, as surely as it is the first time a baby gets its hands on a match.

His wife was a high-spirited woman; and would have been hard to handle at times if it had not been for the fact that she was foolish enough to love him. Since he did not love her at all, it was consequently both simple and practical to terminate all quarrels by dropping out of sight for several days until her obvious fear of losing him for good brought her to a proper humility. He took good care, each time he disappeared, to pick some new and secure hiding place where past experience or her several years' knowledge of his habits would be no help in locating him. Actually, he enjoyed thinking up new and undiscoverable bolt-holes, and made a hobby out of discovering them.

Consequently, he was in high spirits the grey winter afternoon he descended unannounced on the weather station of Burke McIntyre, high in the Lonesome Mountains, a jagged, kindless chain on the deserted shorelands of

3

Venus' Northern Sea. He had beaten a blizzard to the dome with minutes to spare; and now, with his small two-place flier safely stowed away, and a meal of his host's best supplies under his belt, he sat revelling in the comfort of his position and listening to the hundred-and-fifty-per-hour, subzero winds lashing impotently at the arching roof overhead.

"Ten minutes more," he said to Burke, "and I'd have had a tough time making it."

"Tough!" snorted Burke. He was a big, heavy-featured blond man with a kindly contempt for all of of humanity aside from the favored class of meteorologists. "You Lowlanders are too used to that present day Garden of Eden you have down below. Ten minutes more and you'd have been spread over one of the peaks around here to wait for the spring searching party to gather your bones."

Cary laughed in cheerful disbelief.

"Try it, if you don't believe me," said Burke. "No skin off my nose if you don't have the sense to listen to reason. Take your bug up right now if you want."

"Not me." Cary's brilliant white teeth flashed in his swarthy face. "I know when I'm comfortable. And that's no way to treat your guest, tossing him out into the storm when he's just arrived."

"Some guest," rumbled Burke. "I shake hands with you after the graduation exercises, don't hear a word from you for six years and then suddenly you're knocking at my door here in the hinterland."

"I came on impulse," said Cary. "It's the prime rule of my life. Always act on impulse, Burke. It puts the sparkle in existence."

"And leads you to an early grave," Burke supplemented.

"If you have the wrong impulses," said Cary. "But then if you get sudden urges to jump off cliffs or play Russian Roulette then you're too stupid to live, anyway."

"Cary," said Burke heavily, "you're a shallow thinker."

"And you're a stodgy one," grinned Cary. "Suppose

you quit insulting me and tell me something about yourself. What's this hermit's existence of yours like? What do you do?''

"What do I do?" repeated Burke. "I work."

"But just how?" Cary said, settling himself cosily back into his chair. "Do you send up balloons? Catch snow in a pail to find how much fell? Take sights on the stars? Or what?"

Burke shook his head at him and smiled tolerantly.

"Now what do you want to know for?" he asked. "It'll just go in one ear and out the other."

"Oh, some of it might stick," said Cary. "Go ahead, anyhow."

"Well, if you insist on my talking to entertain you," he answered, "I don't do anything so picturesque. I just sit at a desk and prepare weather data for transmission to the Weather Center down at Capital City."

"Aha!" Cary said, waggling a lazy forefinger at him in reproof. "I've got you now. You've been lying down on the job. You've the only one here; so if you don't take observations, who does?"

"You idiot!" said Burke. "The machine does, of course. These stations have a Brain to do that."

"That's worse," Cary answered. "You've been sitting here warm and comfortable while some poor little Brain scurries around outside in the snow and does all your work for you."

"Oh, shut up!" Burke said. "As a matter of fact you're closer to the truth than you think; and it wouldn't do you any harm to learn a few things about the mechanical miracles that let you lead a happy ignorant life. Some wonderful things have been done lately in the way of equipping these stations."

Cary smiled mockingly.

"I mean it," Burke went on, his face lighting up. "The Brain we've got here now is the last word in that type of installation. As a matter of fact, it was just put in recently—up until a few months back we had to work with a job that was just a collector and computer. That is, it collected the weather data around this station and presented it to you. Then you had to take it and prepare it for the calculator, which would chew on it for a while and then pass you back results which you again had to prepare for transmission downstairs to the Center.''

"Fatiguing, I'm sure," murmured Cary, reaching for the drink placed handily on the end table beside his chair. Burke ignored him, caught up in his own appreciation of the mechanical development about which he was talking.

"It kept you busy, for the data came in steadily; and you were always behind since a batch would be accumulating while you were working up the previous batch. A station like this is the center-point for observational mechs posted at points over more than five hundred square miles of territory; and, being human, all you had time to do was skim the cream off the reports and submit a sketchy picture to the calculator. And then there was a certain responsibility involved in taking care of the station and yourself.

"But now"—Burke leaned forward determinedly and stabbed a thick index finger at his visitor—"we've got a new installation that takes the data directly from the observational mechs—all of it—resolves it into the proper form for the calculator to handle it, and carries it right on through to the end results. All I still have to do is prepare the complete picture from the results and shoot it downstairs.

"In addition, it runs the heating and lighting plants, automatically checks on the maintenance of the station. It makes repairs and corrections on verbal command and has a whole separate section for the consideration of theoretical problems.''

"Sort of a little tin god," said Cary, nastily. He was used to attention and subconsciously annoyed by the fact that Burke seemed to be waxing more rhapsodic over his machine than the brilliant and entertaining guest who, as far as the meteorologist could know, had dropped in under the kind impulse to relieve a hermit's boring existence.

Unperturbed, Burke looked at him and chuckled.

"No," he replied. "A *big* tin god, Cary."

The lawyer stiffened slightly in his chair. Like most people who are fond of poking malicious fun at others, he gave evidence of a very thin skin when the tables were turned.

"Sees all, knows all, tells all, I suppose," he said sarcastically. "Never makes a mistake. Infallible."

"You might say that," answered Burke, still with a grin on his face. He was enjoying the unusual pleasure of having the other on the defensive. But Cary, adept at verbal battles, twisted like an eel.

"Too bad, Burke," he said. "But those qualities alone don't quite suffice for elevating your gadget to godhood. One all-important attribute is lacking—invulnerability. Gods never break down."

"Neither does this."

"Come now, Burke," chided Cary, "you mustn't let your enthusiasm lead you into falsehood. No machine is perfect. A crossed couple of wires, a burned out tube and where is your darling? Plunk! Out of action."

Burke shook his head.

"There aren't any wires," he said. "It uses beamed connections. And as for burned out tubes, they don't even halt consideration of a problem. The problem is just shifted over to a bank that isn't in use at the time; and automatic repairs are made by the machine itself. You see, Cary, in this model, no bank does one specific job, alone. Any one of them—and there's twenty, half again as many as this station would ever need—can do any job from running the heating plant to operating the calculator. If something comes up that's too big for one bank to handle, it just hooks in one or more of the idle banks—and so on until it's capable of dealing with the situation."

"Ah," said Cary, "but what if something *did* come up that required all the banks and more too? Wouldn't it overload them and burn itself out?"

"You're determined to find fault with it, aren't you, Cary," answered Burke. "The answer is no. It wouldn't. Theoretically it's possible for the machine to bump into a problem that would require all or more than all of its banks to handle. For example, if this station suddenly popped into the air and started to fly away for no discernible reason, the bank that first felt the situation would keep reaching out for help until all the banks were engaged in considering it, until it crowded out all the other functions the machine performs. But, even then, it wouldn't overload and burn out. The banks would just go on considering the problem until they had evolved a theory that explained why we were flying through the air and what to do about returning us to our proper place and functions.''

Cary straightened up and snapped his fingers.

''Then it's simple,'' he said. ''I'll just go in and tell your machine—on the verbal hookup—that we're flying through the air.''

Burke gave a sudden roar of laughter.

''Cary, you dope!'' he said. ''Don't you think the men who designed the machine took the possibility of verbal error into account? You say that the station is flying through the air. The machine immediately checks by making its own observations; and politely replies, 'Sorry, your statement is incorrect' and forgets the whole thing.''

Cary's eyes narrowed and two spots of faint color flushed the tight skin over his cheekbones; but he held his smile.

''There's the theoretical section,'' he murmured.

''There is,'' said Burke, greatly enjoying himself, ''and you could use it by going in and saying 'consider the false statement or data—this station is flying through the air' and the machine would go right to work on it.''

He paused, and Cary looked at him expectantly.

''But—'' continued the meteorologist, triumphantly, ''it would consider the statement with only those banks not then in use; and it would give up the banks whenever a section using real data required them.''

He finished, looking at Cary with quizzical good humor. But Cary said nothing; only looked back at him as a weasel might look back at a dog that has cornered it against the wall of a chicken run.

''Give up, Cary,'' he said at last. ''It's no use.

Neither God nor Man nor Cary Harmon can interrupt my Brain in the rightful performance of its duty.''

And Cary's eyes glittered, dark and withdrawn beneath their narrowed lids. For a long second, he just sat and looked, and then he spoke.

"I could do it," he said, softly.

"Do what?" asked Burke.

"I could gimmick your machine," said Cary.

"Oh, forget it!" boomed Burke. "Don't take things so seriously, Cary. What if you can't think of a monkey wrench to throw into the machinery? Nobody else could, either."

"I said I could do it," repeated Cary.

"Once and for all," answered Burke, "it's impossible. Now stop trying to pick flaws in something guaranteed flawless and let's talk about something else."

"I will bet you," said Cary, speaking with a slow, steady intensity, "five thousand credits that if you leave me alone with your machine for one minute I can put it completely out of order."

"Forget it, will you?" exploded Burke. "I don't want to take your money, even if five thousand *is* the equivalent of a year's salary for me. The trouble with you is, Cary, you never could stand to lose at anything. Now forget it!"

"Put up or shut up," said Cary.

Burke took a deep breath.

"Now look," he said, the beginnings of anger rumbling in his deep voice. "Maybe I did wrong to needle you about the machine. But you've got to get over the idea that I can be bullied into admitting that you're right. You've got no conception of the technology that's behind the machine, and no idea of how certain I am that you, at least, can't do anything to interfere with its operation. You think that there's a slight element of doubt in my mind and that you can bluff me out of proposing an astronomical bet. Then, if I won't bet, you'll tell yourself you've won. Now listen, I'm not just ninety-nine point nine, nine, nine, nine, per cent sure of myself. I'm one hundred per cent sure of myself and the reason I won't bet you is because that would be robbery; and besides, once you'd lost, you'd hate me for winning the rest of your life.''

"The bet still stands," said Cary.

"All right!" roared Burke, jumping to his feet. "If you want to force the issue, suit yourself. It's a bet."

Cary grinned and got up, following him out of the pleasant, spacious sitting room, where warm lamps dispelled the grey gloom of the snow-laden sky beyond the windows, and into a short, metal-walled corridor where the ceiling tubes blazed in efficient nakedness. They followed this for a short distance to a room where the wall facing the corridor and the door set in it were all of glass.

Here Burke halted.

"There's the machine," he said, pointing through the transparency of the wall and turning to Cary behind him. "If you want to communicate with it verbally, you speak into that grille there. The calculator is to your right; and that inner door leads down to the room housing the lighting and heating plants. But if you're thinking of physical sabotage, you might as well give up. The lighting and heating systems don't even have emergency controls. They're run by a little atomic pile that only the machine can be trusted to handle—that is, except for an automatic setup that damps the pile in case lightning strikes the machine or some such thing. And you couldn't get through the shielding in a week. As for breaking through to the machine up here, that panel in which the grille is set is made of two-inch-thick steel sheets with their edges flowed together under pressure."

"I assure you," said Cary. "I don't intend to damage a thing."

Burke looked at him sharply, but there was no hint of sarcasm in the smile that twisted the other's thin lips.

"All right," he said, stepping back from the door. "Go ahead. Can I wait here, or do you have to have me out of sight?"

"Oh, by all means, watch," said Cary. "We machine-gimmickers have nothing to hide." He turned mockingly to Burke, and lifted his arms. "See? Nothing up my right sleeve. Nothing up my left."

"Go on," interrupted Burke roughly. "Get it over with. I want to get back to my drink."

"At once," said Cary, and went in through the door, closing it behind him.

Through the transparent wall, Burke watched him approach the panel in line with the speaker grille and stop some two feet in front of it. Having arrived at this spot, he became utterly motionless, his back to Burke, his shoulders hanging relaxed and his hands motionless at his sides. For the good part of a minute, Burke strained his eyes to discover what action was going on under the guise of Cary's apparent immobility. Then an understanding struck him and he laughed.

"Why," he said to himself, "he's bluffing right up to the last minute, hoping I'll get worried and rush in there and stop him."

Relaxed, he lit a cigarette and looked at his watch. Some forty-five seconds to go. In less than a minute, Cary would be coming out, forced at last to admit defeat—that is, unless he had evolved some fantastic argument to prove that defeat was really victory. Burke frowned. It was almost pathological, the way Cary had always refused to admit the superiority of anyone or anything else; and unless some way was found to soothe him he would be a very unpleasant companion for the remaining days that the storm held him marooned with Burke. It would be literally murder to force him to take off in the tornado velocity winds and a temperature that must be in the minus sixties by this time. At the same time, it went against the meteorologist's grain to crawl for the sake of congeniality—

The vibration of the generator, half-felt through the floor and the soles of his shoes, and customarily familiar as the motion of his own lungs, ceased abruptly. The fluttering streamers fixed to the ventilator grille above his head ceased their colorful dance and dropped limply down as the rush of air that had carried them, ceased. The lights dimmed and went out, leaving only the grey and ghostly light from the thick windows at each end of the corridor to illuminate the passage and the room. The cigarette dropped unheeded from Burke's fingers and in two swift strides he was at the door and through it.

"What have you done?" he snapped at Cary.

The other looked mockingly at him, then walked across to the nearer wall of the room and leaned his shoulder blades negligently against it.

"That's for you to find out," he said, his satisfaction clearly evident.

"Don't be insane—" began the meteorologist. Then, checking himself like a man who has no time to lose, he whirled on the panel and gave his attention to the instruments on its surface.

The pile was damped. The ventilating system was shut off and the electrical system was dead. Only the power in the storage cells of the machine itself was available for the operating light still glowed redly on the panel. The great outside doors, wide enough to permit the ingress and exit of a two-man flier, were closed, and would remain that way, for they required power to open or close them. Visio, radio, and teletype were alike, silent and lifeless through lack of power.

But the machine still operated.

Burke stepped to the grille and pressed the red alarm button below it, twice.

"Attention," he said. "The pile is damped and all fixtures besides yourselves lack power. Why is this?"

There was no response, though the red light continued to glow industriously on the panel.

"Obstinate little rascal, isn't it?" said Cary from the wall.

Burke ignored him, punching the button again, sharply.

"Reply!" he ordered. "Reply at once! What is the difficulty? Why is the pile not operating?"

There was no answer.

He turned to the calculator and played his fingers expertly over the buttons. Fed from the stored power within the machine, the punched tape rose in a fragile white arc and disappeared through a slot in the panel. He finished his punching and waited.

There was no answer.

For a long moment he stood there, staring at the calculator as if unable to believe that, even in this last hope, the machine had failed him. Then he turned slowly and faced Cary.

"What have you done?" he repeated dully.

"Do you admit you were wrong?" Cary demanded.

"Yes," said Burke.

"And do I win the bet?" persisted Cary gleefully.

"Yes."

"Then I'll tell you," the lawyer said. He put a cigarette between his lips and puffed it alight; then blew out a long streamer of smoke which billowed out and hung cloudily in the still air of the room, which, lacking heat from the blowers, was cooling rapidly. "This fine little gadget of yours may be all very well at meteorology, but it's not very good at logic. Shocking situation, when you consider the close relationship between mathematics and logic."

"What did you do?" reiterated Burke hoarsely.

"I'll get to it," said Cary. "As I say, it's a shocking situation. Here is this infallible machine of yours, worth, I suppose, several million credits, beating its brains out over a paradox."

"A paradox!" the words from Burke were almost a sob.

"A paradox," sang Cary, "a most ingenious paradox." He switched back to his speaking voice. "Which, in case you don't know, is from Gilbert and Sullivan's 'Pirates of Penzance.' It occurred to me while you were bragging earlier that while your little friend here couldn't be damaged, it might be immobilized by giving it a problem too big for its mechanical brain cells to handle. And I remembered a little thing from one of my pre-law logic courses—an interesting little affair called Epimenides Paradox. I don't remember just how it was originally

13

phrased—those logic courses were dull, sleepy sort of businesses, anyway—but for example, if I say to you 'all lawyers are liars' how can you tell whether the statement is true or false, since I am a lawyer and, if it is true, must be lying when I say that all lawyers are liars? But, on the other hand, if I am lying, then all lawyers are not liars, and the statement is false, i.e., a lying statement. If the statement is false, it is true, and if true, false, and so on, so where are you?''

Cary broke off suddenly into a peal of laughter.

"You should see your own face, Burke," he shouted. "I never saw anything so bewildered in my life—anyway, I just changed this around and fed it to the machine. While you waited politely outside, I went up to the machine and said to it, 'You must reject the statement I am now making to you, because all the statements are incorrect.' ''

He paused and looked at the meteorologist.

"Do you see, Burke? It took that statement of mine in and considered it for rejecting. But it could not reject it without admitting that it was correct, and how could it be correct when it stated that all statements I made were incorrect. You see . . . yes, you do see, I can see it in your face. Oh, if you could only look at yourself now. The pride of the meteorology service, undone by a paradox.''

And Cary went off into another fit of laughter that lasted for a long minute. Every time he would start to recover, a look at Burke's wooden face, set in lines of utter dismay, would set him off again. The meteorologist neither moved, nor spoke, but stared at his guest as if he were a ghost.

Finally, weak from merriment, Cary started to sober up. Chuckling feebly, he leaned against the wall, took a deep breath and straightened up. A shiver ran through him, and he turned up the collar of his tunic.

"Well," he said. "Now that you know what the trick was, Burke, suppose you get your pet back to its proper duties again. It's getting too cold for comfort and that daylight coming through the windows isn't the most cheerful thing in the world, either."

But Burke made no move toward the panel. His eyes were fixed and they bored into Cary as unmovingly as before. Cary snickered a little at him.

"Come on, Burke," he said. "Man the pumps. You can recover from your shock sometime afterward. If it's the bet that bothers you, forget it. I'm too well off myself to need to snatch your pennies. And if it's the failure of Baby here, don't feel too bad. It did better than I expected. I thought it would just blow a fuse and quit working altogether, but I see it's still busy and devoting every single bank to obtaining a solution. I should imagine"—Cary yawned—"that it's working toward evolving a theory of types. *That* would give it the solution. Probably could get it, too, in a year or so."

Still Burke did not move. Cary looked at him oddly.

"What's wrong?" he asked irritatedly.

Burke's mouth worked, a tiny speck of spittle flew from one corner of it.

"You—" he said. The word came tearing from his throat like the hoarse grunt of a dying man.

"What—"

"You fool!" groaned out Burke, finding his voice. "You stupid idiot! You insane moron!"

"Me? Me?" cried Cary. His voice was high in protest, almost like a womanish scream. "I was right!'

"Yes, you were right," said Burke. "You were too right. How am I supposed to get the machine's mind off this problem and on to running the pile for heat and light, when all its circuits are taken up in considering your paradox? What can *I* do, when the Brain is deaf, and dumb and blind?"

The two men looked at each other across the silent room. The warm breath of their exhalations made frosty plumes in the still air; and the distant howling of the storm deadened by the thick walls of the station, seemed to grow louder in the silence, bearing a note of savage triumph.

The temperature inside the station was dropping very fast—

The Star-Fool

No one knows who first pinned that unkind name upon the wandering scholars of the galaxy but it is not hard to guess from what class of men he came. Undoubtedly he was some one of the pioneering element, miner, merchant, middleman, or any of the other various groups that tore into the endless planetary frontier during the twenty-eighth century. To these men, exploitation, pure and simple, was the only worthwhile occupation. They looked with contemptuous scorn on the geologists, archeologists, paleontologists, all those whose aim was the acquisition of pure knowledge.

Consequently, there was a certain amount of ironic humor in a situation that arose on Krynor IV near the close of the twenty-eighth century. It began when an epidemic of nerve-disease broke out among the pioneering element there. It grew when the officials of the Federation Government tried to get in touch with their medical station on Tarn II, where the remedy for that particularly virulent plague was cultured in a serum made from native blood. They were answered by the ravings of a madman. And it reached its peak of humorous irony when those same officials discovered that the only human within reasonable distance of the station was a star-fool, an insignificant little geologist by the name of Peter Whaley . . .

* * *

It is not true that every man must have some kind of companion if he is going to wander the depths of space. There are some few self-sufficient individuals who find the company of their work quite sufficient, and, in fact, prefer it to the society of their own kind. Peter Whaley was one of these. A young man with an addiction to sloppy, comfortable clothes and a distaste for combing his hair, he had not the slightest objection to company—when he was not busy. When he was busy, the existence of the rest of the human race was superfluous.

At the present moment, on the airless moon of Tarn II, he was busy.

"George," he said, gazing into the large scanner set into one wall of his control-room, "bring me a specimen from that large black boulder to your right."

Fifty miles away, a small robot chirped an acknowledgement of the order, rolled, hopped and jumped to the boulder in question, and excised a small chunk of it. Having done so, it tucked the specimen into a place in its body and chirped again to signify that the specimen was secured.

"Very good, George," said Peter Whaley, approvingly. "Now bring all the specimens you've got back to the ship."

The little robot chirped and began to roll. Peter turned away from the screen. No need to watch further. George was the last word in specimen-collectors, and could be relied on to return safely over any kind of terrain.

He was laying out his apparatus for chemical analysis, when the deep-space communicator buzzed. With a puzzled frown, he laid down the test-tube he was holding and walked over to the communicator screen, switched it on.

There was a second of blurring motion as the tubes warmed; then the features of Rad Dowell, Commissioner, Thirty-Ninth Galactic Sector, spring into sharp relief on the screen. To Peter, who had seen them twice before during news space-casts, they were only vaguely familiar, as the face of someone known a long time ago.

"Whaley, geologist, speaking," said Peter, automatically. There was a long pause as his voice and image crossed lightyears of distance, to Thirty-Ninth Headquarters on Tynan V. Then the image in the ships' screen spoke again.

"Rad Dowell, Sector Commissioner, calling," said the grey-haired man in the dark blue uniform of a Federation official. "Are you at present on the moon of Tarn II?"

"I am," answered Peter. "There is a black basalt here which, in my opinion, is decidedly unusual for a moon of this type. Not only its prevalence, but its peculiar structure reflect a kind of igneous action in the local strata—" He broke off noticing a look of exasperation on the Commissioner's lined face. "I beg your pardon," he said. "What did you call me about?"

The commissioner sighed. The words star-fool were so obviously passing through his mind that they might as well have been printed on the screen. This, then, was the only man available to handle a crisis that meant life or death to literally millions.

"Whaley," said the Commissioner, heavily, "do you know what nerve disease is?"

"No, I don't," answered Peter, truthfully.

"It's a virus infection that strikes humans whose natural resistance has been lowered by exposure to cosmic radiation," explained the older man. "If we catch it in time, we can cure it—with the proper serum. The only difficulty is that it has a three-month incubation period and can only be detected during the last two or three weeks of that period. Since it is highly infectious, that means that by the time an epidemic breaks into the open, it has usually spread over half a dozen or more planets and thousands of people are already infected. That means that when an epidemic does break out, we have to rush serum immediately to all possible danger points and start general inoculations. Whaley, we have an epidemic on our hands right now—

and that planet below you is the galaxy's only source of serum!''

And, swiftly, the Commissioner outlined the situation to Peter Whaley.

"You are not government personnel," he wound up. "You have absolutely no training in handling alien races and the situation down there is probably dangerous as hell. I can't order you to go, and I don't know what you can do if you do go. All I can do is ask—will you?"

It was quite a question.

Peter Whaley, geologist, looked at his chemical apparatus spread out on the workbench, and thought of the little robot skittering back over the moon's airless surface even now. That was his work, not this. What could he do, if he went, seeing that he was without training and without experience? Barring a minor miracle he would probably do no more than make a ridiculous mess of things and die a stupid death. And the Lord only knew what he would find down there.

But, when he opened his mouth to refuse, a sudden irrational pride mixed with anger came swelling up in his throat like a bubble to choke off his words. Wasn't he, after all, as good as the next man, as good as these hard-headed empire builders? Abruptly a tingling urge for adventure ran hotly through his veins, and he threw logic and common sense together to the winds.

"Of course, Commissioner," he said. "I'll leave right away."

Surprise and hope mixed themselves for a moment in the expression on Rad Dowell's face.

"Good man!" he answered. "There's a ship on the way from here to pick up the serum. See if you can have a load ready for them when they get there. Every day's delay means several thousand lives. And—good luck."

"Thanks," said Peter, feeling suddenly embarrassed, and cut the connection.

For a moment he stood, bemused, until an insistent chirping brought him from his trance and set him to opening the airlock. The little robot had hit a stretch of smooth rock and made good time on the way back. Peter closed the outer lock, opened the inner, and the squat mechanical rolled in, blinking its red toplight furiously in warning that it was still too cold from exposure to airless space to be safely touched.

"It's all right, George," said Peter, wryly. "We won't be getting to work on those samples for quite some time. Just dump them into the storage bin and get ready for takeoff."

George turned and wheeled off in the direction of the storage bin, and Peter settled himself at the controls. Actually, although it was not really necessary with the almost automatic ship he drove, Peter was a better than average pilot and he procrastinated a little, checking various dials and indicators until there was no longer any real excuse for delaying the takeoff. When there was no more reason for delay, he sighed once, cleared his tubes with a short blast, and took off.

From above, the station looked like a small colony of ant-hills. Only the metallic sheen of the domed huts and the signal tower denied the impression. There was no answer to Peter's beamed announcement of landing; and neither human nor alien stirred in the clearing. He cut his power and dropped to the baked clay of the landing spot.

Still, nothing moved. Peter sat at the silent controls and wondered. The first emergency call from Sector Headquarters, they said, had been answered by a blank screen from which came senseless ravings in a voice which could no longer be identified as one of the station members. Since then, the station had not answered at all. The question was: was the madman still alive and waiting for Peter, someplace out there?

Peter rubbed his nose, thoughtfully. Inside him, a cold little voice was regretting his hasty acceptance of the Commissioner's request. What are you doing here? the voice was asking. This is not your line of business. Leave adventure for the men who are trained for it. At the same time, however, an innate stubborness rose up to combat

21

his uneasiness. Peter had the dogged persistence character-
istic of his kind, and he had never yet abandoned, unfin-
ished, a job to which he had committed himself. Madman
or not, it was necessary that Peter investigate the station.
Consequently, there was no point in delaying further.

He rose from the controls and put on an air-helmet.
Then, from a dusty and almost forgotten locker, he dug
out an explosive pellet handgun and clipped it to his belt.
This done, he activated the airlocks, keyed them for re-
entrance, and went out into the clearing.

Outside the ship, he headed for the nearest cone,
which was the communications-shack. His visual image,
checked by the automatic scanner and passed as human,
opened the door before him, and he stepped inside.

Within, the body of a man lay sprawled before the
deep-space communicator. His skull had been crushed from
behind, and the evidence of the blood dried brown on the
floor and the partial decay of his body bore witness that he
had been dead for some time.

Peter looked around without touching anything; then
went back outside and continued his search through the
other buildings. It was as he had suspected. No living
human remained in the station. Only five silent bodies.
And of these, four had been murdered and one was a
suicide.

He returned to the communications-shack and called
Sector Headquarters.

"Well?" asked Rad Dowell, as soon as his face
appeared on the screen.

"How many men," asked Peter, "were here at the
station?"

"Five," answered the Commissioner. "One psychol-
ogist, three medical technicians, and the station chief, a
sort of medical administrator and contact man with the
natives."

"They're all dead," said Peter, and went on to recite
what he had seen. "Evidently one of the technicians went
insane and was confined to the infirmary. Somehow he
killed his attendant, broke out and killed the rest of the

men, and then hung himself. There's evidence of a struggle in the infirmary, but all the others were killed evidently without warning."

The lines on the Commissioner's face deepened.

"And the serum?" he asked. "It should be in the storehouse next to the culture lab?"

"I checked," answered Peter. "The storehouse is empty."

Incredulity replaced the worry etched on the Commissioner's features. "Empty?" he said. "You mean that the drums in the storehouse are empty?"

"I mean there are no drums," Peter informed him.

"But where could they have gone to?" said the Commissioner, bewilderedly. "There must be drums . . . And some of them must contain serum! Find out where they've gone to, Whaley. Ask the natives. There's a translator in the main office that'll make you intelligible to them."

Peter set his jaw.

"There are no natives," he said.

In the screen the Commissioner seemed to sag within his uniform.

"There's hundreds sick here," he said, in a hollow voice, "and nobody knows how many more infected that don't know it yet. On the frontier planets where it started, twenty per cent of the population are dying. And all those people have their hopes pinned on a ship which is on its way to you to pick up the serum that should be stored there. And now you tell me that there isn't any." There was something almost pathetic in the tone of his concluding words.

Peter looked steadily at him.

"What do you want me to do?" he asked.

"I don't know," said Rad Dowell. "Find the drums. They must be somewhere. There must be some serum in them. If you can't do that—" his voice trailed off on a note of hopelessness—"wait until the ship comes, I suppose. Perhaps—"

But what the rest of his sentence was, Peter never heard. For at that moment, there was the crash of a heavy body striking the wall of the communications-shack, and the set went dead. The abrupt violence shocked him into a momentary paralysis. For a second he stood there, staring stupidly at the screen as if he expected it to light up again of its own accord. Then, when the patent absurdity of this had penetrated his mind, he reacted swiftly with an action that was as foolish as it was brave. Unclipping the hand-gun from his belt, he walked to the door with it held in his right hand, and stepped out into the open.

"Halt!"

For a second, the scene had all the appearance of a tableau. There was Peter, brought to an abrupt halt by what he saw, the pellet gun upraised in one hand, and there was the cause of the disturbance, a group of Tarnian natives, frozen, holding the treetrunk they had been using as a battering ram on the tower of the communications-shack.

"Halt," he said again, foolishly, for of course it meant nothing to the Tarnians.

After that things began to happen quickly.

The natives, losing their nerve at the actual appearance of the human they had been threatening, dropped the treetrunk and went bounding in great kangeroo-like hops for the forest at the edge of the clearing. Peter yelled—a quite meaningless and thoroughly instinctive battle-sound—and fired the gun at random. The pellets streamed from its muzzle at ten-thousand feet per second, missed the natives by a wide margin, and blew some fifty square meters of the forest beyond to smoking fragments. The natives, convinced that their doom was inescapably upon them, skidded to a halt and stood, their large, fish-like eyes rolling in terror, antennae quivering, too frightened to either advance into the devastated area or return toward Peter.

"Halt!" yelled Peter, a wild exhilaration filling him at finding himself in command of the situation. "Don't move. I'll be right back."

He might as well have spoken in Sanskrit for all the natives understood but the command was unnecessary.

Nothing short of an earthquake could have moved the Tarnian raiding party at that moment.

Peter ducked hurriedly into the main office building, picked up the translator—a dark colored box with two adjustable helmets attached—and ducked out again. He walked up to the raiding party and dropped the "alien" helmet on the antennaed head of the first squat green creature he came to. Then he put the "human" helmet on his own head and switched on the power.

"Who's in charge here?" Peter demanded.

"Not this one, Lord, not this one," chattered the earphones terriffiedly in his ear. "This one loves the lords. This one was made to come here by that one chief—" and a trembling green paw indicated a scowling Tarnian who was glaring at Peter's informant with murder in his eyes.

"Ha!" said Peter. He lifted the "alien" helmet from the head of the one he had been talking to, walked over, and dumped it on the native indicated.

"Are you the chief?"

"This one chief," was the sullen acknowledgement.

"Why did you break the communications tower?" Peter asked.

"Don't want tower," growled the native.

"Why not?"

"This one tower not tree. Break down. This one lord not Tarn-man. Go away."

"Just as I thought," said Peter grimly. "So you were trying to scare me off. Well, I don't scare. What made you decide that you didn't want humans here?"

"Lords take Tarn-blood. Those ones Lords say these ones Tarn-men give blood and those ones Lords protect Tarn-men from devils. Those ones Lords lie."

"Oh?" said Peter. "And what made you think they lied?"

"Those ones lords dead long time now. No devils."

Peter grimaced a trifle wryly.

The native's logic was simple but definite enough. He thought fast.

"Did it ever occur to you," he said, "that something might still be protecting you from devils?"

"Yes."

The answer stopped Peter. He blinked.

"Oh?" he said. "Who, then?"

"The old gods," was the complacent and surprising answer. "The spirit who lives in the village idols protects those ones villages."

Peter shook his head inside the helmet. This kind of crisis in native-human relations called for a trained administrator. Best to let it ride until the ship got here. But there was one thing he could do.

"In that one building," he said, slipping into the Tarnian phraseology, and indicating the storehouse, "were a lot of large metal drums. Where are they?"

"These ones take," answered the native.

"Bring them back!" snapped Peter.

"Gods say no," returned the other stubbornly. "Those ones drums have Tarn-blood in them."

"But it isn't Tarn-blood any longer, you fool," said Peter desperately. "It's serum."

"Tarn-blood," repeated the native doggedly. "Sacred."

Peter stared at him. The frustrations, he thought, must be making him ill. A strange sort of dizziness made his head swim. Abruptly, he lost all control of his temper—

"Bring them back, damn you!" he screamed, lashing out with his fist at the small native. "Bring them back!"

The native ducked, and the helmet flopped from his head. Finding himself free, he began to run. The others bolted after him, and in a second the clearing was empty, except for Peter.

Dizzily, he turned and headed back toward his ship. Have to report this, he thought, and, with the communications-shack out of order, the only transmitter was aboard his vessel. His emotions seemed oddly difficult to control. Once he turned about in a sudden fit of rage and, screaming curses, sent a stream of pellets to explode into the forest where the Tarnians had disappeared. Then he made his way into the ship and switched on his set, calling Sector Headquarters.

The face of Rad Dowell took form on the screen.

"Hello, Whaley," the Commissioner said. "Any luck?"

"Why should I have luck?" asked Peter, sourly. "The natives are trying to break away from human control. They've reverted to worship of their village idols. They've stolen the serum from the storehouse and won't bring it back."

Rad Dowell shook his head despairingly.

"It looks hopeless," he said.

"Of course it's hopeless," snapped Peter. "You knew that when you sent me here."

The Commissioner's eyes narrowed suddenly; he looked suspiciously at Peter.

"Tell me, Whaley," he asked, "you had inoculations yourself before you left for the Tarn moon, didn't you?"

"What inoculations?" demanded Peter.

"Why—Tarn itself is the home of the nerve disease!" said the Commissioner. "I thought you knew that. That's why the native blood can be used as a culture for the preventive serum. Only on Tarn it's that much worse, because while the disease runs for the regular two weeks through alternate periods of excitement and lassitude before it kills the patient, there's no incubation period required if you catch it directly from a native carrier. But you must have been inoculated before they gave your ship clearance papers for Tarn from your last stop."

Peter looked at him dully.

"I didn't have clearance papers for Tarn," he replied. "Just for the moon of Tarn." He paused. Somewhere within him, a thick black vein of anger pulsed and throbbed feverishly; the screen in front of him seemed to shake in time with its beating. Then, abruptly, it rose like a fiery tide inside him and rage spewed words from his mouth.

"You knew it!" he screamed, as the walls of the ship spun crazily about him. "You sent me to my death. To my death! *To my death!*" And, whipping the handgun from

27

his belt, he sent it crashing, butt first, directly into the screen.

There was an instantaneous flash of intense, blue-violet light, and the set went dead.

"If you want my opinion, Cushey—" began third-mate Ron Parker.

"Which I don't," interrupted the little doctor, bristling.

"As I say," continued the young officer, imperturbably, "if you want my opinion, he's already dead; and we two are going to look like damn fools, leaping off the ship the minute she lands and rushing up to a corpse with revivicator and half the medical equipment the City of Parth carries on board."

He looked moodily out the airlock scanner, watching the medical station of Tarn II float up to them as the big government-ship eased in for a landing.

"And what if he isn't, hey?" barked Major Cushey. "What if there's a flicker of life left in him and we can bring him back enough to tell us something of what's been going on around here . . . what if he finally found out where the drums are kept, hey? Isn't a thousand to one chance worth a little physical effort, even to you, if it means halting an epidemic? Lazy young lout!"

"Not lazy. Just no point in expecting—" Ron began. A slight jar announced that they had grounded. "Oh, well, here we go, ready or not—" and the two men flipped their air-helmets down over their heads and clipped them tight.

Before them, the outer lock swung open. They leaped out and hit the ground running, Major Cushey bouncing ahead like a particularly energetic, if overfed rabbit, and Ron loping clumsily along behind, the long, awkward bulk of the revivicator clutched lovingly to his chest.

"Try the office building first," Cushey's voice shrilled in the young officer's earphones. Ron cursed and followed the shorter man to the building with the Federation flag flying above it. They reached it. The scanner, noting their speed, checked them hastily, and the door swung open. They plunged inside . . .

. . . And skidded to a shocked and startled halt. For rising from a chair to greet them, unsteady, pale, but undeniably alive, was the man they had come to save.

"You'll excuse me for not going outside to meet the ship," he said. "I heard you landing, but I'm a little too weak to walk that far yet."

They stared at him.

"But you're not sick!" said Cushey peevishly, as if it were rather unkind of Peter to be alive at all.

"Not any more," answered Peter, sinking back in his chair.

"How did this happen, this—this cure," barked the little doctor.

"In the most ordinary way," said Peter, "I took some of the serum."

"But you told the Commissioner the natives had taken all the serum there was."

"They had," said Peter. He closed his eyes and chuckled. "I—er—persuaded them to bring it back. The storehouse is full of drums of it right now—a full load for you to take back."

The two officers looked at each other.

"Pardon me," said Cushey, and stepped forward to curl two fingers over Peter's pulse.

Peter chuckled again. "No, I'm quite well," he said. "Look in the storehouse if you don't believe me."

"But how could you do it?" cried Ron . . . *a star-fool, like you!* his words implied.

"Simple," answered Peter. "They thought that their village idols were ample protection against devils—that they didn't need human protection. So I supplied them with a devil that their idols were no protection against. They came crying to me for help. I tottered out into the clearing, challenged It, and when It showed up, blew It to bits." He paused, "After that, they fell over themselves to be good to me. Brought the serum back, and offered to bleed all over the place for me—'course I couldn't take them up on that, not knowing how to make the serum. But when you're ready for them, I can whistle them up in a jiffy."

"But I still don't understand," protested the bewildered Ron. "What was the devil? Where would you get a devil?"

"The devil?" echoed Peter. "Oh, that was George, my specimen collector. Poor George. I hated to blow him to pieces, but it was him or me."

"Specimen collector?" repeated the medical major in an odd tone of voice, applying his stethoscope to Peter's chest. "But I know what they are. They're just small robots that chip off pieces of rock and bring them to you for examination. Ruggedly built, of course; but I don't see what devil-like aspects one of those could have. Your George was utterly harmless."

Peter laughed out loud. And this time he opened his eyes and looked them both full in the face.

"Not," he said, cheerfully, "when he went around on my orders collecting specimens from all of the village idols, he wasn't."

Hilifter

It was locked—from the outside.

Not only that, but the mechanical latch handle that would override the button lock on the tiny tourist cabin aboard the *Star of the North* was hidden by the very bed on which Cully When sat cross-legged, like some sinewy mountain man out of Cully's own pioneering ancestry. Cully grinned at the image in the mirror which went with the washstand now hidden by the bed beneath him. He would not have risked such an expression as that grin if there had been anyone around to see him. The grin, he knew, gave too much of him away to viewers. It was the hard, unconquerable humor of a man dealing for high stakes.

Here, in the privacy of this locked cabin, it was also a tribute to the skill of the steward who had imprisoned him. A dour and cautious individual with a long Scottish face, and no doubt the greater part of his back wages reinvested in the very spaceship line he worked for. Or had Cully done something to give himself away? No. Cully shook his head. If that had been the case, the steward would have done more than just lock the cabin. It occurred to Cully that his face, at last, might be becoming known.

"I'm sorry, sir," the steward had said, as he opened the cabin's sliding door and saw the unmade bed. "Off-watch steward's missed making it up." He clucked reprovingly. "I'll fix it for you, sir."

"No hurry," said Cully. "I just want to hang my clothes; and I can do that later."

"Oh, no, sir." The lean, dour face of the other—as primitive in a different way as Cully's own—looked shocked. "Regulations. Passenger's gear to be stowed and bunk made up before overdrive."

"Well, I can't just stand here in the corridor," said Cully. "I want to get rid of the stuff and get a drink." And indeed the corridor was so narrow, they were like two vehicles on a mountain road. One would have to back up to some wider spot to let the other past.

"Have the sheets in a moment, sir," said the steward. "Just a moment, sir. If you wouldn't mind sitting up on the bed, sir?"

"All right," said Cully. "But hurry. I want to step up for a drink in the lounge."

He hopped up on to the bed, which filled the little cabin in its down position; and drew his legs up tailor-fashion to clear them out of the corridor.

"Excuse me, sir," said the steward, closed the door, and went off. As soon as he heard the button lock latch, Cully had realized what the man was up to. But an unsuspecting man would have waited at least several minutes before hammering on the locked door and calling for someone to let him out. Cully had been forced to sit digesting the matter in silence.

At the thought of it now, however, he grinned again. That steward was a regular prize package. Cully must remember to think up something appropriate for him, afterward. At the moment, there were more pressing things to think of.

Cully looked in the mirror again and was relieved at the sight of himself without the betraying grin. The face that looked back at him at the moment was lean and angular. A little peroxide solution on his thick, straight brows, had taken the sharp appearance off his high cheekbones and given his pale blue eyes a faintly innocent expression. When he really wanted to fail to impress sharply discerning eyes, he also made it a point to chew gum.

The present situation, he considered now, did not call for that extra touch. If the steward was already even vaguely suspicious of him, he could not wait around for an ideal opportunity. He would have to get busy now, while they were still working the spaceship out of the solar system to a safe distance where the overdrive could be engaged without risking a mass-proximity explosion.

And this, since he was imprisoned so neatly in his own shoebox of a cabin, promised to be a problem right from the start.

He looked around the cabin. Unlike the salon cabins on the level overhead, where it was possible to pull down the bed and still have a tiny space to stand upright in—either beside the bed, in the case of single-bed cabins, or between them, in the case of doubles—in the tourist cabins once the bed was down, the room was completely divided into two spaces—the space above the bed and the space below. In the space above, with him, were the light and temperature and ventilation controls, controls to provide him with soft music or the latest adventure tape, food and drink dispensers and a host of other minor comforts.

There were also a phone and a signal button, both connected with the steward's office. Thoughtfully he tried both. There was, of course, no answer.

At that moment a red light flashed on the wall opposite him; and a voice came out of the grille that usually provided the soft music.

"We are about to maneuver. This is the Captain's Section, speaking. We are about to maneuver. Will all lounge passengers return to their cabins? Will all passengers remain in their cabins, and fasten seat belts. We are about to maneuver. This is the Captain's Section—"

Cully stopped listening. The steward would have known this announcement was coming. It meant that everybody but crew members would be in their cabins and crew members would be up top in control level at maneuver posts. And that meant nobody was likely to happen along to let Cully out. If Cully could get out of this cabin, however, those abandoned corridors could be a break for him.

However, as he looked about him now, Cully was rapidly revising downward his first cheerful assumption that he—who had gotten out of so many much more intentional prisons—would find this a relatively easy task. On the same principle that a pit with unclimbable walls and too deep to jump up from and catch an edge is one of the most perfect traps designable—the tourist room held Cully. He was on top of the bed; and he needed to be below it to operate the latch handle.

First question: How impenetrable was the bed itself? Cully dug down through the covers, pried up the mattress, peered through the springs, and saw a blank panel of metal. Well, he had not really expected much in that direction. He put the mattress and covers back and examined what he had to work with above-bed.

There were all the control switches and buttons on the wall, but nothing among them promised him any aid. The walls were the same metal paneling as the base of the bed. Cully began to turn out his pockets in the hope of finding something in them that would inspire him. And he did indeed turn out a number of interesting items, including a folded piece of notepaper which he looked at rather soberly before laying it aside, unfolded, with a boy scout type of knife that just happened to have a set of lock picks among its other tools. The note would only take up valuable time at the moment, and—the lock being out of reach in the door—the lock picks were no good either.

There was nothing in what he produced to inspire him, however. Whistling a little mournfully, he began to make the next best use of his pile of property. He unscrewed the nib and cap of his long, gold fountain pen, took out the ink cartridge and laid the tube remaining aside. He removed his belt, and the buckle from the belt. The buckle, it appeared, clipped on to the fountain pen tube in somewhat the manner of a pistol grip. He reached in his mouth, removed a bridge covering from the second premolar to the second molar, and combined this with a small metal throwaway dispenser of the sort designed to contain antacid tablets. The two together had a remarkable resemblance to the magazine and miniaturized trigger assembly of a small handgun; and when he attached them to the buckle-fountain-pen-tube combination the resemblance became so marked as to be practically inarguable.

Cully made a few adjustments in this and looked around himself again. For the second time, his eye came to rest on the folded note, and, frowning at himself in the mirror, he did pick it up and unfold it. Inside it read: "O wae the pow'r the Giftie gie us" Love, Lucy. Well, thought Cully, that was about what you could expect from a starry-eyed girl with Scottish ancestors, and romantic notions about present-day conditions on Alderbaran IV and the other new worlds.

". . . But if you have all that land on Asterope IV, why aren't you back there developing it?" she had asked him.

"The New Worlds are stifling to death," he had answered. But he saw then she did not believe him. To her, the New Worlds were still the romantic Frontier, as the Old Worlds Confederation newspapers capitalized it. She thought he had given up from lack of vision.

"You should try again . . ." she murmured. He gave up trying to make her understand. And then, when the cruise was over and their shipboard acquaintance—that was all it was, really—ended on the Miami dock, he had felt her slip something in his pocket so lightly only someone as self-trained as he would have noticed it. Later he had found it to be this note—which he had kept now for too long.

He started to throw it away, changed his mind for the sixtieth time and put it back in his pocket. He turned back to the problem of getting out of the cabin. He looked it over, pulled a sheet from the bed and used its length to measure a few distances.

The bunk was pivoted near the point where the head of it entered the recess in the wall that concealed it in Up position. Up, the bunk was designed to fit with its foot next to the ceiling. Consequently, coming up, the foot would describe an arc—

About a second and a half later he had discovered that the arc of the foot, ascending, would leave just enough space in the opposite top angle between wall and ceiling so that if he could just manage to hang there, while releasing the safety latch at the foot of the bed, he might be able to get the bed up past him into the wall recess.

It was something which required the muscle and skill normally called for by so-called "chimney ascents" in mountain climbing—where the climber wedges himself between two opposing walls of rock. A rather wide chimney—since the room was a little more than four feet in width. But Cully had had some little experience in that line.

He tried it. A few seconds later, pressed against walls and ceiling, he reached down, managed to get the bed released, and had the satisfaction of seeing it fold up by him. Half a breath later he was free, out in the corridor of the Tourist Section.

The corridor was deserted and silent. All doors were closed. Cully closed his own thoughtfully behind him and went along the corridor to the more open space in the center of the ship. He looked up a steel ladder to the entrance of the Salon Section, where there would be another ladder to the Crew Section, and from there eventually to his objective—the Control level and the Captain's Section. Had the way up those ladders been open, it would have been simple. But level with the top of the ladder he saw the way to the Salon section was closed off by a metal cover capable of withstanding fifteen pounds per square inch of pressure.

It had been closed, of course, as the other covers would have been, at the beginning of the maneuver period.

Cully considered it thoughtfully, his fingers caressing the pistol grip of the little handgun he had just put together. He would have preferred, naturally, that the covers be open and the way available to him without the need for fuss or muss. But the steward had effectively ruled out that possibility by reacting as and when he had. Cully turned away from the staircase, and frowned, picturing the layout of the ship, as he had committed it to memory five days ago.

There was an emergency hatch leading through the ceiling of the end tourist cabin to the end salon cabin overhead, at both extremes of the corridor. He turned and went down to the end cabin nearest him, and laid his finger quietly on the outside latch-handle.

There was no sound from inside. He drew his put-together handgun from his belt; and, holding it in his left hand, calmly and without hesitation, opened the door and stepped inside.

He stopped abruptly. The bed in here was, of course, up in the wall, or he could never have entered. But the cabin's single occupant was asleep on the right-hand seat of the two seats that an upraised bed left exposed. The occupant was a small girl of about eight years old.

The slim golden barrel of the handgun had swung immediately to aim at the child's temple. For an automatic second, it hung poised there, Cully's finger half-pressing the trigger. But the little girl never stirred. In the silence, Cully heard the surge of his own blood in his ears and the faint crackle of the note in his shirt pocket. He lowered the gun and fumbled in the waistband of his pants, coming up with a child-sized anesthetic pellet. He slipped this into his gun above the regular load, aimed the gun, and fired. The child made a little uneasy movement all at once; and then lay still. Cully bent over her for a second, and heard the soft sound of her breathing. He straightened up. The pellet worked not through the blood stream, but immediately through a reaction of the nerves. In fifteen minutes the effect would be worn off, and the girl's sleep would be natural slumber again.

He turned away, stepped up on the opposite seat and laid his free hand on the latch handle of the emergency hatch overhead. A murmur of voices from above made him hesitate. He unscrewed the barrel of the handgun and put it in his ear with the other hollow end resting against the ceiling which was also the floor overhead. The voices came, faint and distorted, but understandable to his listening.

". . . Hilifter," a female voice was saying.

"Oh, Patty!" another female voice answered. "He was just trying to scare you. You believe everything."

"How about that ship that got hilifted just six months ago? That ship going to one of the Pleiades, just like this one? The *Queen of Argyle*—"

"Princess of Argyle."

"Well, you know what I mean. Ships do get hilifted. Just as long as there're governments on the pioneer worlds that'll license them and no questions asked. And it could just as well happen to this ship. But you don't worry about it a bit."

"No, I don't."

"When hilifters take over a ship, they kill off everyone who can testify against them. None of the passengers or ship's officers from the *Princess of Argyle* was ever heard of again."

"Says who?"

"Oh, everybody knows that!"

Cully took the barrel from his ear and screwed it back onto his weapon. He glanced at the anesthetized child and thought of trying the other cabin with an emergency hatch. But the maneuver period would not last more than twenty minutes at the most and five of that must be gone already. He put the handgun between his teeth, jerked the latch to the overhead hatch, and pulled it down and open.

He put both hands on the edge of the hatch opening; and with one spring went upward into the salon cabin overhead.

He erupted into the open space between a pair of facing seats, each of which held a girl in her twenties. The one on his left was a rather plump, short, blond girl who was sitting curled up on her particular seat with a towel across her knees, an open bottle of pink nail polish on the towel, and the brush-cap to the bottle poised in her hand.

The other was a tall, dark-haired, very pretty lass with a lap-desk pulled down from the wall and a handscriber on the desk where she was apparently writing a letter. For a moment both stared at him, and his gun; and then the blonde gave a muffled shriek, pulled the towel over her head and lay still, while the brunette, staring at Cully, went slowly pale.

"Jim!" she said.

"Sorry," said Cully. "The real name's Cully When. Sorry about this, too, Lucy." He held the gun casually, but it was pointed in her general direction. "I didn't have any choice."

A little of the color came back. Her eyes were as still as fragments of green bottle glass.

"No choice about what?" she said.

"To come through this way," said Cully. "Believe me, if I'd known you were here, I'd have picked any other way. But there wasn't any other way; and I didn't know."

"I see," she said, and looked at the gun in his hand. "Do you have to point that at me?"

"I'm afraid," said Cully, gently, "I do."

She did not smile.

"I'd still like to know what you're doing here," she said.

"I'm just passing through," said Cully. He gestured with the gun to the emergency hatch to the Crew Section, overhead. "As I say, I'm sorry it has to be through your cabin. But I didn't even know you were serious about emigrating."

"People usually judge other people by themselves," she said expressionlessly. "As it happened, I believed you." She looked at the gun again. "How many of you are there on board?"

"I'm afraid I can't tell you that," said Cully.

"No. You couldn't, could you?" Her eyes held steady on him. "You know, there's an old poem about a man like you. He rides by a farm maiden and she falls in love with him, just like that. But he makes her guess what he is; and she guesses . . . oh, all sorts of honorable things, like soldier, or forester. But he tells her in the end he's just an outlaw, slinking through the wood."

Cully winced.

"Lucy—" he said. "Lucy—"

"Oh, that's all right," she said. "I should have known when you didn't call me or get in touch with me, after the boat docked." She glanced over at her friend, motionless under the towel. "You have the gun. What do you want us to do?"

"Just sit still," he said. "I'll go on up through here and be out of your way in a second. I'm afraid—" he reached over to the phone on the wall and pulled its cord loose. "You can buzz for the steward, still, after I'm gone," he said. "But he won't answer just a buzzer until after the maneuver period's over. And the stairway hatches are locked. Just sit tight and you'll be all right."

He tossed the phone aside and tucked the gun in the waistband.

"Excuse me," he said, stepping up on the seat beside her. She moved stiffly away from him. He unlatched the hatch overhead, pulled it down; and went up through it. When he glanced back down through it, he saw her face stiffly upturned to him.

He turned away and found himself in an equipment room. It was what he had expected from the ship's plans he had memorized before coming aboard. He went quickly out of the room and scouted the Section.

As he had expected, there was no one at all upon this level. Weight and space on interstellar liners being at the premium that they were, even a steward like the one who had locked him in his cabin did double duty. In overdrive, no one but the navigating officer had to do much of anything. But in ordinary operation, there were posts for all ships personnel, and all ships personnel were at them up in the Captain's Section at Control.

The stair hatch to this top and final section of the ship, he found to be closed as the rest. This, of course, was routine. He had not expected this to be unlocked, though a few years back ships like this might have been that careless. There were emergency hatches from this level as well, of course, up to the final section. But it was no part of Cully's plan to come up in the middle of a Control room or a Captain's Section filled with young, active, and almost certainly armed officers. The inside route was closed.

The outside route remained a possibility. Cully went down to the opposite end of the corridor and found the entry port closed, but sealed only by a standard lock. In an adjoining room there were outside suits. Cully spent a few minutes with his picks, breaking the lock of the seal; and then went in to put on the suit that came closest to fitting his six-foot-two frame.

A minute later he stepped out onto the outside skin of the ship.

As he watched the outer door of the entry port closing ponderously in the silence of airless space behind him, he felt the usual inner coldness that came over him at times like this. He had a mild but very definite phobia about open space with its myriads of unchanging stars. He knew what caused it—several psychiatrists had told him it was nothing to worry about, but he could not quite accept their unconcern. He knew he was a very lonely individual, underneath it all; and subconsciously he guessed he equated space with the final extinction in which he expected one day to disappear and be forgotten forever. He could not really believe it was possible for someone like him to make a dent in such a universe.

It was symptomatic, he thought now, plodding along with the magnetic bootsoles of his suit clinging to the metal hull, that he had never had any success with women—like Lucy. A sort of bad luck seemed to put him always in the wrong position with anyone he stood a chance of loving. Inwardly, he was just as starry-eyed as Lucy, he admitted to himself, alone with the vastness of space and the stars, but he'd never had much success bringing it out into the open. Where she went all right, he seemed to go all wrong. Well, he thought, that was life. She went her

41

way and he would go his. And it was probably a good thing.

He looked ahead up the side of the ship, and saw the slight bulge of the observation window of the navigator's section. It was just a few more steps now.

Modern ships were sound insulated, thankfully, or the crew inside would have heard his dragging footsteps on the hull. He reached the window and peered in. The room he looked into was empty.

Beside the window was a small, emergency port for cleaning and repairs of the window. Clumsily, and with a good deal of effort, he got the lock-bolt holding it down unscrewed, and let himself in. The space between outer and inner ports here was just enough to contain a spacesuited man. He crouched in darkness after the outer port had closed behind him.

Incoming air screamed up to audibility. He cautiously cracked the interior door and looked into a room still empty of any crew members. He slipped inside and snapped the lock on the door before getting out of his suit.

As soon as he was out, he drew the handgun from his belt and cautiously opened the door he had previously locked. He looked out on a short corridor leading one way to the Control Room, and the other, if his memory of the memorized ship plans had not failed him, to the central room above the stairway hatch from below. Opening off this small circular space surrounding the hatch, would be another entrance directly to the Control Room, a door to the Captain's Quarters, and one to the Communications Room.

The corridor was deserted. He heard voices coming down it from the Control Room; and he slipped out the door that led instead to the space surrounding the stairway hatch. And checked abruptly.

The hatch was open. And it had not been open when he had checked it from the level below, ten minutes before.

For the first time he cocked an ear specifically to the kinds of voices coming from the Control Room. The acoustics of this part of the ship mangled all sense out of the words being said. But now that he listened, he had no trouble recognizing, among others, the voice of Lucy.

It occurred to him then with a kind of wonder at himself, that it would have been no feat for an active girl like herself to have followed him up through the open emergency hatch, and later mount the crew level stairs to the closed hatch there and pound on it until someone opened up.

He threw aside further caution and sprinted across to the doorway of the Captain's Quarters. The door was unlocked. He ducked inside and looked around him. It was empty. It occurred to him that Lucy and the rest of the ship's complement would probably still be expecting him to be below in the Crew's section. He closed the door and looked about him, at the room he was in.

The room was more lounge than anything else, being the place where the captain of a spaceship did his entertaining. But there was a large and businesslike desk in one corner of the room, and in the wall opposite, was a locked, glassed-in case holding an assortment of rifles and handguns.

He was across the room in a moment and in a few, savage, seconds, had the lock to the case picked open. He reached in and took down a short-barreled, flaring-muzzled riot gun. He checked the chamber. It was filled with a full thousand-clip of the deadly steel darts. Holding this in one hand and his handgun in the other, he went back out the door and toward the other entrance to the control room— the entrance from the central room around the stairway hatch.

". . . He wouldn't tell me if there were any others," Lucy was saying to a man in a captain's shoulder tabs, while eight other men, including the dour-faced steward who had locked Cully in his cabin, stood at their posts, but listening.

"There aren't any," said Cully, harshly. They all turned to him. He laid the handgun aside on a control table by the entrance to free his other hand, and lifted the heavy riot gun in both hands, covering them. "There's only me."

"What do you want?" said the man with the captain's tabs. His face was set, and a little pale. Cully ignored the question. He came into the room, circling to his right, so as to have a wall at his back.

"You're one man short," said Cully as he moved. "Where is he?"

"Off-shift steward's sleeping," said the steward who had locked Cully in his room.

"Move back," said Cully, picking up crew members from their stations at control boards around the room, and herding them before him back around the room's circular limit to the very entrance by which he had come in. "I don't believe you."

"Then I might as well tell you," said the captain, backing up now along with Lucy and the rest. "He's in Communications. We keep a steady contact with Solar Police right up until we go into overdrive. There are two of their ships pacing alongside us right now, lights off, a hundred miles each side of us."

"Tell me another," said Cully. "I don't believe that either." He was watching everybody in the room, but what he was most aware of were the eyes of Lucy, wide upon him. He spoke to her, harshly. "Why did you get into this?"

She was pale to the lips; and her eyes had a stunned look.

"I looked down and saw what you'd done to that child in the cabin below—" her voice broke off into a whisper. "Oh, Cully—"

He laughed mournfully.

"Stop there," he ordered. He had driven them back into a corner near the entrance he had come in. "I've got to have all of you together. Now, one of you is going to tell me where that other man is—and I'm going to pick you off, one at a time until somebody does."

"You're a fool," said the captain. A little of his color had come back. "You're all alone. You don't have a chance of controlling this ship by yourself. You know what happens to Hilifters, don't you? It's not just a prison sentence. Give up now and we'll all put in a word for you. You might get off without mandatory execution."

"No thanks," said Cully. He gestured with the end of the riot gun. "We're going into overdrive. Start setting up the course as I give it to you."

"No," said the captain, looking hard at him.

"You're a brave man," said Cully. "But I'd like to point out something. I'm going to shoot you if you won't co-operate; and then I'm going to work down the line of your officers. Sooner or later somebody's going to preserve his life by doing what I tell him. So getting yourself killed isn't going to save the ship at all. It just means somebody with less courage than you lives. And you die."

There was a sharp, bitter intake of breath from the direction of Lucy. Cully kept his eyes on the captain.

"How about it?" Cully asked.

"No brush-pants of a colonial," said the captain, slowly and deliberately, "is going to stand in my Control Room and tell me where to take my ship."

"Did the captain and officers of the *Princess of Argyle* ever come back?" said Cully, somewhat cryptically.

"It's nothing to me whether they came or stayed."

"I take it all back," said Cully. "You're too valuable to lose." The riot gun shifted to come to bear on the First Officer, a tall, thin, younger man whose hair was already receding at the temples. "But you aren't, friend. I'm not even going to tell you what I'm going to do. I'm just going to start counting; and when I decide to stop you've had it. One . . . two . . ."

"Don't! Don't shoot!" The First Officer jumped across the few steps that separated him from the Main Computer Panel. "What's your course? What do you want me to set up—"

The captain began to curse the First Officer. He spoke slowly and distinctly and in a manner that completely ignored the presence of Lucy in the Control Room. He went right on as Cully gave the First Officer the course and the First Officer set it up. He stopped only, as—abruptly—the lights went out, and the ship overdrove.

When the lights came on again—it was a matter of only a fraction of a second of real time—the captain was at last silent. He seemed to have sagged in the brief interval of darkness and his face looked older.

And then, slamming through the tense silence of the room came the sound of the Contact Alarm Bell.

"Turn it on," said Cully. The First Officer stepped over and pushed a button below the room's communication screen. It cleared suddenly to show a man in a white jacket.

"We're alongside, Cully," he said. "We'll take over now. How're you fixed for casualties?"

"At the moment—" began Cully. But he got no further than that. Behind him, three hard, spaced words in a man's voice cut him off.

"Drop it, Hilifter!"

Cully did not move. He cocked his eyebrows a little sadly and grinned his untamable grin for the first time at the ship's officers, and Lucy and the figure in the screen. Then the grin went away.

"Friend," he said to the man hidden behind him. "Your business is running a spaceship. Mine is taking them away from people who run them. Right now you're figuring how you make me give up or shoot me down and this ship dodges back into overdrive, and you become a hero for saving it. But it isn't going to work that way."

He waited for a moment to hear if the off-watch steward behind him—or whoever the officer was—would answer. But there was only silence.

"You're behind me," said Cully. "But I can turn pretty fast. You may get me coming around, but unless you've got something like a small cannon, you're not going to stop me getting you at this short range, whether you've got me or not. Now, if you think I'm just talking, you better think again. For me, this is one of the risks of the trade."

He turned. As he did so he went for the floor; and heard the first shot go by his ear. As he hit the floor another shot hit the deck beside him and ricocheted into his side. But by that time he had the heavy riot gun aimed and he pressed the firing button. The stream of darts knocked the man backward, out of the entrance to the control room to lie, a still and huddled shape, in the corridor outside.

Cully got to his feet, feeling the single dart in his side. The room was beginning to waver around him, but he felt that he could hold on for the necessary couple of minutes before the people from the ship moving in alongside could breach the lock and come aboard. His jacket was loose and would hide the bleeding underneath. None of those facing him could know he had been hit.

"All right, folks," he said, managing a grin. "It's all over but the shouting—" And then Lucy broke suddenly from the group and went running across the room toward the entrance through which Cully had come a moment or so earlier.

"Lucy—" he barked at her. And then he saw her stop and turn by the control table near the entrance, snatching up the little handgun he had left there. "Lucy, do you want to get shot?"

But she was bringing up the little handgun, held in the grip of both her hands and aiming it squarely at him. The tears were running down her face.

"It's better for you, Cully—" she was sobbing. "Better . . ."

He swung the riot gun to bear on her, but he saw she did not even see it.

"Lucy, I'll have to kill you!" he cried. But she no more heard him, apparently, than she saw the muzzle-on view of the riot gun in his hands. The wavering golden barrel in her grasp wobbled to bear on him.

"Oh, Cully!" she wept. "Cully—" And pulled the trigger.

"Oh, *hell!*" said Cully in despair. And let her shoot him down.

*   *   *

When he came back, things were very fuzzy there at first. He heard the voice of the man in the white jacket, arguing with the voice of Lucy.

"Hallucination—" muttered Cully. The voices broke off.

"Oh, he said something!" cried the voice of Lucy.

"Cully?" said the man's voice. Cully felt a two-finger grip on his wrist in the area where his pulse should be—if, that was, he had a pulse. "How're you feeling?"

"Ship's doctor?" muttered Cully, with great effort. "You got the *Star of the North?*"

"That's right. All under control. How do you feel?"

"Feel fine," mumbled Cully. The doctor laughed.

"Sure you do," said the doctor. "Nothing like being shot a couple of times and having a pellet and a dart removed to put a man in good shape."

"Not Lucy's fault—" muttered Cully. "Not understand." He made another great effort in the interests of explanation. "Stars'n eyes."

"Oh, what does he mean?" wept Lucy.

"He means," said the voice of the doctor harshly, "that you're just the sort of fine young idealist who makes the best sort of sucker for the sort of propaganda the Old World's Confederation dishes out."

"Oh, you'd say that!" flared Lucy's voice. "Of course, you'd say that!"

"Young lady," said the doctor, "how rich do you think our friend Cully, here, is?"

Cully heard her blow her nose, weakly.

"He's got millions, I suppose," she said, bitterly. "Hasn't he hilifted dozens of ships?"

"He's hilifted eight," said the doctor, dryly, "which, incidentally, puts him three ships ahead of any other contender for the title of hilifting champion around the populated stars. The mortality rate among single workers—and you can't get any more than a single 'lifter aboard Confederation ships nowadays—hits ninety per cent with the third ship captured. But I doubt Cully's been able to save many millions on a salary of six hundred a month, and a bonus of one tenth of one per cent of salvage value, at Colonial World rates.''

There was a moment of profound silence.

''What do you mean?'' said Lucy, in a voice that wavered a little.

''I'm trying,'' said the doctor, ''for the sake of my patient—and perhaps for your own—to push aside what Cully calls those stars in your eyes and let a crack of surface daylight through.''

''But why would he work for a salary—like that?'' Disbelief was strong in her voice.

''Possibly,'' said the doctor, ''just possibly because the picture of a bloodstained hilifter with a knife between his teeth, carousing in Colonial bars, shooting down Confederation officers for the fun of it, and dragging women passengers off by the hair, has very little to do with the real facts of a man like Cully.''

''Smart girl,'' managed Cully. ''S'little mixed up, s'all—'' He managed to get his vision cleared a bit. The other two were standing facing each other, right beside his bed. The doctor had a slight flush above his cheekbones and looked angry. Lucy, Cully noted anxiously, was looking decidedly pale. ''Mixed up—'' Cully said again.

''Mixed up isn't the word for it,'' said the doctor angrily, without looking down at him. ''She and all ninety-nine out of a hundred people on the Old Worlds.'' He went on to Lucy. ''You met Cully Earthside. Evidently you liked him there. He didn't strike you as the scum of the stars, then.

''But all you have to do is hear him tagged with the name 'hilifter' and immediately your attitude changes.''

Lucy swallowed.

''No,'' she said, in a small voice, ''it didn't . . . change.''

''Then who do you think's wrong—you or Cully?'' The doctor snorted. ''If I have to give you reasons, what's the use? If you can't see things straight for yourself, who can help you? That's what's wrong with all the people back on the Old Worlds."

"I believe Cully," she said. "I just don't know why I should."

"Who has lots of raw materials—the raw materials to support trade—but hasn't any trade?" asked the doctor.

She frowned at him.

"Why . . . the New Worlds haven't any trade on their own," she said. "But they're too undeveloped yet, too young—"

"Young? There's three to five generations on most of them!"

"I mean they haven't got the industry, the commercial organization—" she faltered before the slightly satirical expression on the doctor's face. "All right, then, you tell me! If they've got everything they need for trade, why don't they? The Old Worlds did; why don't you?"

"In what?"

She stared at him.

"But the Confederation of the Old Worlds already has the ships for interworld trade. And they're glad to ship Colonial products. In fact they do," she said.

"So a load of miniaturized surgical power instruments made on Asterope in the Pleiades, has to be shipped to Earth and then shipped clear back out to its destination on Electra, also in the Pleiades. Only by the time they get there they've doubled or tripled in price, and the difference is in the pockets of Earth shippers."

She was silent.

"It seems to me," said the doctor, "that girl who was with you mentioned something about your coming from Boston, back in the United States on Earth. Didn't they have a tea party there once? Followed by a revolution? And didn't it all have something to do with the fact that England at that time would not allow its colonies to own and operate their own ships for trade—so that it all had to be funneled through England in English ships to the advantage of English merchants?"

"But why can't you build your own ships?" she said. Cully felt it was time he got in on the conversation. He cleared his throat, weakly.

"Hey—" he managed to say. They both looked at him; but he himself was looking only at Lucy.

"You see," he said, rolling over and struggling up on one elbow, "the thing is—"

"Lie down," said the doctor.

"Go jump out the air lock," said Cully. "The thing is, honey, you can't build spaceships without a lot of expensive equipment and tools, and trained personnel. You need a spaceship-building industry. And you have to get the equipment, tools, and people from somewhere else to start with. You can't get 'em unless you can trade for 'em. And you can't trade freely without ships of your own, which the Confederation, by forcing us to ship through them, makes it impossible for us to have.

"So you see how it works out," said Cully. "It works out you've got to have shipping before you can build shipping. And if people on the outside refuse to let you have it by proper means, simply because they've got a good thing going and don't want to give it up—then some of us just have to break loose and go after it any way we can."

"Oh, Cully!"

Suddenly she was on her knees by the bed and her arms were around him.

"Of course the Confederation news services have been trying to keep up the illusion we're sort of half jungle-jims, half wild-west characters," said the doctor. "Once a person takes a good look at the situation on the New Worlds, though, with his eyes open—" He stopped. They were not listening.

"I might mention," he went on, a little more loudly, "while Cully here may not be exactly rich, he does have a rather impressive medal due him, and a commission as Brevet-Admiral in the upcoming New Worlds Space Force. The New Worlds Congress voted him both at their meeting just last week on Asterope, as soon as they'd finished drafting their Statement of Independence—''

But they were still not listening. It occurred to the doctor then that he had better uses for his time—here on this vessel where he had been Ship's Doctor ever since she first lifted into space—than to stand around talking to deaf ears.

He went out, closing the door of the sick bay on the former *Princess of Argyle* quietly behind him.

Counter-Irritant

Premier Joseph MacIntosh leaned back in his swivel-chair, put the tips of his fingers together in front of his nose, and gazed over them with grave disapproval at the stocky young man on the other side of his official desk.

"Now, let's not be hasty," said MacIntosh.

The young man exploded.

"Hasty!" he bellowed. "After fifty years of wishy-washy shilly-shallying milk-and-water appeasement I ask for a little action, and you tell me not to be hasty!" He choked with anger.

"Hasty!" he repeated furiously, pounding the fragile, mirror-like surface of the Premier's desk.

"Yes, Mr. Van Brock," said the Premier firmly, "hasty. It's not a light matter to plunge the Solar System and its colonies into a probably-disastrous war. My policy, and the policy of this government will be, as always, to keep the peace."

"Government policy!" snorted Van Brock. "Poly-Sci partyline policy, you mean."

The Premier looked at him steadily. "Mr. Van Brock," he said. "You're a young representative to the lower house of the United Worlds Government, and a new representative. For that reason you're allowed occasional breaches of decorum that would not be pardoned in an older office-holder. But it might be a good idea to remember that is all you are; and that I am the executive head of this Government. The decision in these cases is mine."

Van Brock leaned forward, gripping the edge of the Premier's desk with both hands. All the tremendous vitality of his personality was concentrated in this one unconscious gesture.

"But don't you understand, sir!" he cried. "Vega's the one big rival we have! She's as strong as we are, and growing stronger." He swung away from the desk and strode over to the three-dimensional star map on the wall.

"Look," he said, extending a finger. "Here's Vega, 26.5 light years away—three months by overdrive. Here's Arcturus, five months away. And here's Altair, only two months away. Where do most of those complaints on your desk come from? Altair. The Vegans are stepping on the toes of our colonists on every inhabitable system we've discovered so far. But if they can get the upper hand on Altair, they'll be practically squatting on our doorstep."

"Don't you think, Mr. Van Brock," said the Premier with just a touch of sarcasm, "that Altairian barbarians would have some objection to Vegan domination?"

"What could they do?" retorted Van Brock. "Even with our help, the barbarian races on Altair are behind the Arcturians. And the Arcturians are just on the threshold of civilization. Both of them are too unhuman to help or hinder. But the Vegans are our natural enemies. They're humanoid; they're intelligent and civilized. We quit too soon in the last war with them; we should have gone on and crushed them entirely."

MacIntosh looked at him. "You weren't alive fifty years ago," he said. "That war was a stalemate. It would have ended by exhausting Earth and Vega races together."

"That's an opinion only."

"It was my opinion," said the Premier, "at the time we signed the peace, and now. You're a chauvinist through ignorance Mr. Van Brock; and I don't intend to see Humanity stretched on the rack of another war simply to educate you."

Van Brock's mouth twisted bitterly. "Don't you see," he said, "that this ostrich-like policy of deliberately ignoring friction between our colonials and Vegan traders, and exploiters on the barbarian worlds, is leading inevitably to this very war you're so frightened of?"

"I do not."

Van Brock sighed heavily. "You force me to take the whole matter to the public," he said.

MacIntosh stood up behind his desk. He stood very straight, in spite of his hundred and fifteen years, and his eyes met Van Brock's on the level at last. "I was put in office, with the rest of the Political Science Party half a century ago, to keep the peace," he said. "And as long as I'm Premier it will be kept. If you want action on Vega, you'll have to get me out."

"All right, then," said Van Brock. "I will."

The Premier smiled a bleak smile.

"And when you've tried that and failed . . ."

"I won't," said Van Brock.

". . . Come back, and have another talk with me."

Van Brock looked at him in some surprise; then shrugged his shoulders, turning away toward the door. "Why not?" he said. "But, as I say, I won't fail." And with that he left the office.

On the steps of Government Head House a thin, wiry-haired little man waited. As Van Brock came out this individual fell into step beside him.

"Well?" the individual asked.

"No luck, Harry," Van Brock answered glumly. "He's honest enough, and human enough, but he's getting old and short-sighted. When he refused to do anything, I threatened to take the whole matter to the public. He challenged me. Said I'd have to get him out of office if I wanted action."

Harry whistled. "That's a stopper," he said.

"Why?" asked Van Brock. "I think I can do it."

"What!" Harry grabbed Van Brock by the arm, swinging him around so that the two men stood halted, facing each other. "Why, you don't have a chance! The Political Science Party has polled a clear majority on every major issue for fifty years, and they'll back MacIntosh to the limit. It's political suicide for a freshman representative like yourself."

Van Brock looked at him a trifle oddly. "I'm not doing this for myself," he said harshly. "It seems to me that the lives of a few billion people are more important than my political career."

"*If* you could do anything for them," said Harry. "*If* these conclusions you've drawn about Vega are true. *If. If.* Come down to earth, Van. I've been a representative's press-agent around Government Center here for nearly three quarters of a century, and I know what I'm talking about. All you'll get out of this will be six month's hard work tying a noose around your own neck."

"And yours, too—is that it?" asked Van Brock bitterly. He gave a short, unhappy laugh. "I don't blame you, Harry. I must be pretty short on persuasion if I can't convince even my own press-agent that there's real danger. Well, I can't get started on this for a couple of weeks at least. I'll help you find another job in that time."

He turned on his heel and walked away.

"Damn fool," said Harry, looking after him.

Van Brock continued to stride off. Suddenly the little man broke into a trot in pursuit.

"Hey, Van," he called. "Slow up. Wait for me."

Two weeks later, the first of Van Brock's broadcasts was aired. There was no advance publicity, but rumor had already spread its reports; a good percentage of those owning reception-boxes on the Three Worlds of Earth, Venus, and Mars, and the colonies listened.

In a billion boxes, then, light swirled, eddied, and coalesced into the thick-shouldered, tri-dimensional image of Van Brock. And his voice came, deep and vibrant, challengingly, to all of them.

"Citizens of the Three Worlds," he said, "men and women of the human race, *we have been betrayed*!"

And, in the office of Premier MacIntosh, a small handful of men listened: middle-aged men; the old guard of the Political Science Party; those who had been present at its victory.

"Young hothead!" grumbled Al Peters, of Extra-Terrestrial Trade Office.

"But dangerous," said another, turning to the Premier. "Don't you think so, Mac?"

Premier MacIntosh, sitting on a couch facing the three-dimensional image in the office reception box and sipping a before-dinner cocktail, looked up at his questioner.

"There's always danger in politics, Joe," he answered. "And Humanity knows we ought to be used to it by now. But I think, in this case, the odds are on our side."

Joe Hennesy, Premier's Aide-de-Camp shrugged, and turned back to the box, from which Van Brock's image was now pouring words in a fiery stream.

"We have been asleep! We have let ourselves be cozened by old men into paying too high a price for peace. We have slumbered in a false security while men in our far-flung colonies in other systems, and on the barbarian worlds, spoke softly and turned the other cheek to Vegan aliens. Men and women alike, of our kind, have bowed down to alien authority; men and women, such as you and I, who call ourselves free and equal to any intelligence in this wide universe.

"And shall I tell you why they have bowed down? Not, fellow humans, because it is their nature to do so. Not because they are naturally servile. Not because they fear the Vegan alien. No, there is another, more shameful reason.

"*It is the law!*

"Yes, it is the law. Our own human law, set up by a bunch of old men whose only policy is—so they say—to keep the peace. But whose peace is this they are keeping?

57

Not the peace of our colonists, who suffer almost constant friction with the Vegans. Not the peace of your children, who—if this goes on—will have to fight Vegan warriors. None of these.

"Men and women of Humanity, I say to you, tonight, from this broadcasting booth in Government Center, that it is *their* peace, and *their* peace alone, that these old men, these political veterans of the Political Science Party, are concerned with. It is the political peace of fifty years following the termination of our last war with Vega that concerns them.

"It is that peace I have broken for you, tonight."

"Whew!" said Joe Hennesy, turning from the reception box. "He's hitting us where it hurts, all right. We can't deny our own watchword. 'To keep the Peace' was the slogan that put us up into office in the first place." He turned for encouragement to the Premier sitting on the couch, who smiled back at him with quiet confidence.

"Take it easy, Joe," said MacIntosh. "We knew somebody like this was bound to come along, sooner or later. He'll whip up a storm all right. But the real test will come when he takes the matter to the Assembly; then we can begin to fight back."

And he smiled again. But he smiled less easily the next day, when liberal newspapers began to clamor for his head.

Van Brock's series of broadcasts went on. He reviewed history for the audience that listened to him. He showed that the forces of Humanity had been holding their own at the time the last peace treaty with Vega was signed. He accused the Political Science Party of taking advantage of a war-weary people to gain office. He charged them with attempting to make cowards out of the human race at the present time, in an effort to hold that office. And he reported incident after incident of Vegan-Human friction in the colonies of the barbarian worlds in the Altairian and Centaurian systems.

"You have heard the facts," he repeated constantly to his listeners. "What do you say to them?"

And, in an ever-increasing volume, in newspapers, in messages to their representatives, they responded that he was right, that the Poly-Scis were wrong, that something must be done.

After some three months of this, a tired MacIntosh said, "Well, Joe, how are things lining up in the Assembly?"

Joe Hennesy winced. "Oh, we've still got our majority in both the upper and lower houses. But I'm afraid it's going to evaporate, the minute Van Brock calls for a vote of confidence in you from the representatives. Once public attention is focused on the houses, it's every man for himself: a lot of our luke-warm members are going to desert to save their own hides."

MacIntosh looked out a window and drummed with his fingers on the top of the desk in front of him. "I didn't expect such a reaction." he murmured, half to himself. "I really didn't."

"It's this younger generation that Van Brock belongs to," said Hennesy. "They're too young to remember the last war, and this talk about old men in office has got them excited."

"And the trouble is," said MacIntosh grimly, "he's right; we *are* old men. But we've got a tiger by the tail and can't let go."

For a minute there was silence in the office. Then Hennesy spoke up again. "Well, chief," he said, finally. "Shall we play it dirty?"

MacIntosh sighed. "I guess we'll have to, Joe," he said. "Fair means or foul, we've got to win; get in touch with Lyt Marja."

Five months to the day from his challenge to MacIntosh, Van Brock received a call from the Vegan Embassy at Government Center.

"Who's this?" he asked sharply.

The light in his communication-box swirled, and the scrawny figure of a Vegan, looking (as all Vegans do) like a half-starved caricature of a human, answered him in a deep bass voice.

"I am Lyt Marja, Mr. Van Brock."

"Well?"

"I think you might find it to your advantage to talk to me."

"Go ahead," said Van Brock.

"No," the Vegan demurred, "not over the public communications system; you must come and see me at the Embassy."

"Nothing doing," said Van Brock. "You boys would like an opportunity to put me out of the way. If you can't talk over the box, you come here."

"Be reasonable, Mr. Van Brock," answered Lyt Marja. "With public excitement at the pitch it is at now, it is somewhat unsafe for a Vegan to venture out. We have been stoned here at the Embassy, and our windows broken. Moreover, for me to visit you would be to announce the matter of our meeting publicly; the result could only be an accusation that our government was meddling in the internal politics of humanity. No, you must come to me—as secretly as possible."

"No thanks," said Van Brock; and broke the connection.

But, after he had ended the conversation, he sat for a while, thinking it over. He did not consider himself to be in ignorance of the motive behind the call. Either it was a bid for the cessation of hostilities being made by the administration, through the safest possible intermediary; or it was an attempt to bribe him off on the part of either the Poly-Sci Party, or the Vegans themselves. As for the personal danger involved in such a visit, both he and the Vegan knew that this was no more than an excuse. Van Brock was far too much in the public eye right now for violence to be a safe measure against him.

He hesitated a minute, biting his lip, wishing that Harry was there to talk the matter over with. Then, making up his mind, he flipped on his communications box and called Lyt Marja back.

"Tonight at ten hundred hours," he said. The Vegan nodded; and Van Brock broke the contact.

It was dark that night when Van Brock slipped up to the Vegan embassy in a car, rented under an assumed name, and rang the bell at the service entrance.

The door opened before him automatically. He entered and it closed behind him. Down a long dark hallway, he could see a door standing ajar and bright light flooding through the opening. He went down the hall.

The door proved to be the entrance to a room comfortably furnished in the human fashion. Cigarettes, and the materials for a drink awaited him. He ignored both and sat down in an armchair to wait.

It was quiet in the room. So quiet, in fact, that he was able to hear the almost noiseless sound of the door closing behind him. His tight nerves jerked him to his feet as the faint click of its latch sounded in his ears. In three swift strides he crossed the room and threw his weight against it.

It was securely locked.

Harry Taylor, returning to the office that was their mutual headquarters, wanted Van Brock. He wanted Van Brock badly, the World Center grapevine had just informed him that a considerable segment of the younger Poly-Sci party group were ready to revolt and come over on Van Brock's side, if that gentleman would spearhead a movement for a general reelection. The little press-agent therefore came bursting into the office with his news on his lips and was quite dumbfounded when he found no one to tell it to.

He glanced hurriedly at Van Brock's check-clock, which showed that the representative had passed out of its reception-area at roughly nine hundred and twenty hours. It was now almost twelve hundred hours. That meant that, according to the rigidly-artificial time of Government Center, which divided the normal twenty-four hours into two thousand units of the same designation, Van Brock had been gone a good quarter of the evening and that it was well past midnight. Harry cursed. Why hadn't Van Brock left a message in plain sight on the automatic secretary? Then the obvious answer that Van might not have wanted his destination broadcast occured to Taylor; he looked anxiously around the room for some less-obvious clue to the representative's whereabouts.

There was little to look at. Government Center offices were fully automatic from dictagraph to disposal chute, and everything was in plain view. Helplessly he checked the blank tapes and blank document sheets in the dicta-graph. They were completely unrewarding. He checked through the filed correspondence that had come in since nine hundred hours; and here also he drew a blank. Finally, his gaze fastened on the relief-image of Government Center on the office wall. If Van Brock was anywhere in the Center, his location would be represented on that map. And if he had meant Harry to know that location, Van Brock would have found some way of marking it un-obtrusively.

Taylor stepped up and began to study the image minutely.

Daylight was beginning to show at the office windows when Taylor found what he wanted: The image of the Vegan Diplomatic House slightly distorted. Eagerly, his fingers probed the imaged building, seeming to disappear as they plunged into the little grey representation. They closed over something hard, and, as he withdrew it, the image snapped back into proper shape again, its reflecting surface being then clear.

The hard object was a tightly-folded pellet of document sheet. He unfolded it and read:

Harry: I'm to meet Lyt Marja for a talk at the Vegan Embassy at ten hundred hours tonight. Don't know about what. If I'm not back in two hundred hours, call out the Marines.

Harry left the office at a dead run.

He broke more than one traffic regulation on the way to the embassy; and he wasted little time once he got there.

Finding the main entrance locked, he tried the service entrance, as Van Brock had done, and was alarmed, rather than reassured, when it opened at his touch. He had taken the pellet-gun from his car holster, and he held it cautiously in front of him as he slipped down the dark corridor.

But there was no opposition waiting, and the door at the far end opened at a touch to reveal an exceedingly angry but unharmed Van Brock sitting in an arm chair. He sprang to his feet as Harry entered.

Harry grunted, midway between overwhelming relief and exasperation.

"What—" he began, but Van Brock cut him short.

"I don't know," he answered. "But let's get out of here fast." And he led the way at a run for Harry's car.

Once they were well away from the embassy, Harry shoved the pellet-gun back into its slot in the dashboard.

"What happened?" he demanded.

Van Brock shook his head and frowned.

"Nothing," he said. "Just exactly nothing. I can't understand it. Lyt Marja may have gotten cold feet at the last minute about telling me whatever it was he wanted to tell me. But then, why keep me locked up? And if I was to be locked up, why let me go when you came?"

"I don't get it either," said Harry. "Did you ever meet this Vegan before?"

"No," said Van Brock. "By the way, what do you know about him, Harry?"

Harry shrugged. "Nothing much. He's one of the older Vegan diplomats. If I remember rightly, he was even part of the peace-signing treaty group that came over here fifty years ago when we ended the war, and opened diplomatic relations with his kind again. For all we know, he may have a lifetime position as ambassador to Government Center. I don't know much about the internal workings of Vegan politics."

"None of us do, blast it," said Van Brock gloomily. "That's another fault we can lay at Poly-Sci's doorstep. Oh, well. Whatever was planned for tonight evidently fell through. So I guess we can forget about it."

* * *

The next morning he woke to find Harry standing over his bed with a face expressive of the worst possible news.

"What's up?" asked Van Brock groggily.

"Everything," said Harry quietly. "Read that." He tossed a newsheet on to Van Brock's bed.

Sleepily, the big man sat up and focused his eyes on the headlines. " 'Van Brock In Secret Communication With Vegan Embassy'," he read out loud. "What . . . ?"

"No point in reading any farther," said Harry. "They've got the whole story of how you went secretly to the Vegan Embassy last night, and the amount of time you spent there. It's just newspaper-talk so far, but I got a call warning me that if you pressed the matter any further there'd be pictures produced and a charge of treason pressed against you."

Van Brock sat stunned. Harry's voice continued, hollow and distant in his ears. "Even if you want to fight the charge, you've already lost the big battle. People are frightened now, and I doubt if you could raise half a dozen votes in the Representatives House to back you after this. There's no alternative to defeat, only degrees of it. Either you give up now, and are simply through with politics; or you keep on going and have a virtually certain conviction of treason pressed against you. And that would mean the death-penalty."

"There's too many people backing me," said Van Brock, dazedly. "Nearly all of humanity is on my side in this question. The government wouldn't dare convict me, let alone execute me."

"Nobody is behind you," said Harry. "The people who listened to you, and agreed with you yesterday, distrust you today. They're afraid of you. They, themselves, would force your conviction and execution if it came to a treason-trial."

There was a long period of silence in the room: and then Harry spoke again. "The Premier wants to see you.

He called and left a message you were to come to him immediately. It's an order.''

In a dream of unreality, Van Brock got up and slipped into his clothes. Harry, watching him, said nothing. Then the representative headed for the door. He was reaching for the latch, when a thought struck him with all the cruelty of an open-handed slap in the face. He turned to look at Harry, who avoided his gaze.

"Harry!" said Van Brock. "*You* don't think I've been hooked up with the Vegans, do you?"

The accusation hung heavy in the room.

"I don't know," said Harry slowly, looking out a window. "I'm inclined to believe you myself; but all I know about what went on last night in the Embassy is what you told me. Then I remember the last war and—I don't know."

Van Brock took a deep breath and went out of the room.

In the Premier's office, MacIntosh awaited him. So did a thin Vegan, whom Van Brock recognized.

"Ah, Van Brock," said MacIntosh. "You've met Lyt Marja."

"Only over a reception-box," answered the young man grimly. "Thanks for the frame, Vegan."

Lyt Marja inclined his head. MacIntosh's lips thinned disapprovingly. "Relax, Van Brock," he said. "What we did was necessary."

"Necessary to what?"

"Necessary to keeping the peace," returned MacIntosh.

Van Brock laughed bitterly. "Did you just get me here to gloat?" he asked. "Because, if so, I'm leaving, protocol or no protocol."

"Not at all," snapped MacIntosh. "You're attributing to us the same sort of childish reactions you're feeling yourself. I asked you here to find out whether you'd like to fill the office of Premier. *My* office, Van Brock."

The words were like a blow to the representative's

solar-plexus. The breath went out of him with a whoosh and he sat down abruptly in a chair. Then he began to laugh a trifle crazily. "What next?" he asked weakly. "Premier?"

"Not right away, of course," said MacIntosh. "But in five or ten years—after this furor has died down and been forgotten. The Poly-Sci party heads have gotten together and decided that you seem to have the kind of qualities we need in the man holding this office. With the party solidly behind you, we can eventually shove you in. We're going to need a new man soon, you know." He smiled a trifle wryly. "You were right, unfortunately when you called us old men."

Van Brock had recovered from his momentary urge to hysteria. He looked straight at the Premier. "This is the most ridiculous thing I ever heard" he said coldly. "Don't you realize that the minute I was in, I'd turn your precious keep the peace policy upside down?"

"No you wouldn't," said MacIntosh.

"Why wouldn't I?" demanded Van Brock.

"Because," said MacIntosh with the suspicion of a smile at the corners of his lips, "in the next five years we should be able to teach you a little common sense."

"Common sense?" Van Brock reared up out of his chair. "What is this you're playing? Some kind of farce?"

"Nonsense," said MacIntosh swiftly. "The Poly-Sci Party has the best reason in the world for acting as it does, although only a handful of we old men at the top know what that reason is. Will you sit still and listen to it?"

"All right," said Van Brock flatly, reseating himself, "go ahead. It must be some whale of a good reason."

"It is," answered MacIntosh. "You came to me six months ago with evidence that the Vegans were moving in and competing with our colonies in the Altairian and Arcturian systems. That evidence was correct. I knew it was correct *because it is what the Poly-Sci Party has been working toward for fifty years*. Listen to a little history, Van Brock."

"The last war with Vega was a stalemate, no matter what our earth histories tell you in your schoolbooks. When the Poly-Sci Party came to power, the war had been going on for forty years, draining the lifeblood of both races. And there was no hope of a solution. Vegans were an expanding, pioneering people; so were humans. The two civilizations were at roughly the same stage of development. Individuals of both races were similar, physically, mentally, and psychologically. We had too many points in common, people said; we were natural enemies.

"What only a few political science theorists recognized was that we were also natural allies.

"But these few intelligences were voices crying in the wilderness. Vegans were killing humans: humans were killing Vegans. It is a hopeless task to preach friendship with a murderer. So, instead, we formed a political party and threw our full weight into obtaining a peace that was little more than a truce, both sides tacitly admitting it was only a breathing-spell to give them time to build up their strength.

"But, having gained a peace, we were determined to keep it."

"And," interjected Van Brock, "merely put off the reckoning until a more bloody day."

"No!" said MacIntosh. "Our job was to put off the reckoning until Vega should come to realize that their eventual well-being rested in a friendly alliance with humans. We set out to bring them to this realization—first by keeping the two races apart, in which we were aided by a few Vegans like Lyt Marja here, who is, himself, the equivalent of a Poly-Sci man on the Vegan worlds; and by supplying a counter-irritant."

"Counter-Irritant?" asked Van Brock.

MacIntosh smiled. "The human race, in spite of a thousand years of contact with alien races, is still unsophisticated in its emotional reaction to aliens. We tend to relate them to our own solar standards; we find it hard to take an

67

alien at face value. Instead, we are likely to assume that because he looks like a teddy bear he must act like a teddy bear—or that because he lives like a mole, he thinks like a mole. In the case of a humanoid, we cannot relate him to an animal; therefore we tend to regard him as an inferior type of human, since a belief in our own superiority is firmly fixed in our minds.

"And the Vegan attitude is the same. Minor differences bulk large in our respective eyes, because we have not yet learned to take each other at face value. Only when races with greater differences begin to claim equality, will these minor differences lose their importance. To bring the Vegans, and even our own people to this realization, the Poly-Sci party has been working to keep the two people apart until pressure from the non-humanoid races on Arcturus and Altair can bring them together. And because the Poly-Sci party is infinitely more strong here on the human worlds than it is on the Vegan, we are the ones who are encouraging trespass by the Vegans on our colonial holdings.

"That's the story Van Brock. What do you think of it?"

There was a moment's silence.

"Why don't you tell this to the people?" asked Van Brock.

"With emotional reactions," answered the Premier, "it's not a matter of telling. Intelligences must be shown."

"Then why are you trying to tell me?"

"Because," said MacIntosh; and again there was the suspicion of a smile at the corners of his mouth. "I think you're just inquisitive enough to go out to Arcturus or Altair and check for yourself on whether there's more common ground between Vegans and humans than there is between either and the barbarian races."

There was a long moment of silence in the Premier's office. Then . . . "I might do just that," said Van Brock, musingly. "I might indeed. But—" he raised his voice, looking up at both MacIntosh and Lyt Marja—"I warn you. No matter what happens to me as a result, if this story doesn't hold water, I'll spread it all over the galaxy among humans and Vegans.''

"Agreed," said MacIntosh.

"Well?" demanded the young man.

Premier Rupert Van Brock leaned back in his swivel chair, put the tips of his fingers together in front of his nose, and gazed over them with grave disapproval.

"Now, let's not be hasty," said Premier Van Brock . . .

Last Voyage

"What's up?" asked Barney Dohouse, the engineer, coming through the hatch and swinging up the three metal steps of the ladder to the control room. Both Jed Alant (the captain), and the young mate Tommy Ris were standing in front of the vision screen.

"We're being followed, Barney," said Jed, without turning around. "Come here and take a look."

The heavy old engineer swung himself forward to stand between the stocky, grizzled captain and the slim young mate. The screen was set on a hundred and eighty degrees rear—which meant it was viewing the segment of space directly behind them. Barney squinted at it. An untrained eye would have seen nothing among the multitude of star points that filled it like an infinite number of gleaming drops from the spatter-brush of an artist; but the engineer, watching closely, made out in the lower left corner of the screen a tiny dark shape that occulted point after glowing point in its progress toward the center of the screen.

The point seemed to crawl with snail-like slowness, but Barney frowned. "Coming up fast, isn't he? Who do you suppose he is?"

"There's no scheduled craft on that course," said Tommy Ris, his blue eyes serious under the carefully combed forelock of his brown hair.

"Uh," grunted Barney. "Think it's Pellies?"

"I'm afraid so." Jed sighed. "And us with passengers."

The three men fell silent, gazing at the screen. It was a reflection on their years of experience in the void that they thought of the passengers rather than themselves. Your true spaceman is a fatalist out of necessity, and as a natural result of having his nose constantly rubbed in the fact that—cosmically speaking—he is not the least bit important. With passengers, as they all three knew, the case was different. Passengers, by and large, are planet-dwellers, comfortably self-convinced of the necessity for their own survival and liable to kick and fuss when the man with the scythe comes along.

The *Tecoatepetl*—*Teakettle* to her friends and crew—had no business carrying passengers in the first place. She had been constructed originally to carry vital drugs and physiological necessities to the pioneer worlds, as soon as they were opened for self-supporting colonists. When the first belt of extra-solar worlds had been supplied, she was already a little outdated. Her atomic power plant and her separate drive section—like one end of a huge dumbell—balanced the control and payload section at the other end of a connecting section like a long tube. Powerful, but not too pretty, she was useful, but not so efficient, by the time sixty years had passed and the hair of her captain and engineer had greyed. As a result she had been downgraded to the carrying of occasional passenger loads—according to the standards of interstellar transportation, where human life is usually slightly less important than cargoes of key materials for worlds who lack them.

Old spaceships never die until something kills them, the demand for anything that will travel between the stars fantastically outweighing the available carrying space. An operating spaceship is worth its weight in—spaceships. To human as well as alien; which was why the non-human ship from the Pleiades was swiftly over-hauling them. Neither humans nor cargo could hold any possible interest for the insectivorous humanoids; but the ship itself was a prize.

"We're five hours from Arcturus Base," said Tommy, "and headed for it at this velocity he can't turn us. Wonder how he figures on getting us past our warships there without being shot up."

"Ask him," said Barney, showing his teeth in a grin.

"You mean—talk to him?" Tommy looked at the captain for permission.

"Why not?" said Jed. "No, wait; I'll do it. Key me in, Tommy."

The younger man seated himself at the transmission board and set himself to locating the distantly-approaching ship with a directional beam. Fifteen minutes later, a green light began to glow and wink like a cat's eye in front of him; and he grunted with satisfaction.

"All yours," he said to Jed. The captain moved over to stand in front of the screen as Tommy turned a dial and the stars faded to give an oddly off-key picture of a red-lighted control room. A tall, supple-looking member of the race inhabiting the Pleiades stars, his short trunk-snout looking like a comic nose stuck in the middle of his elongated face, looked back at him.

"You speak human?" asked Jed.

"I speak it," answered the other. The voice strongly resembled a human's except for a curious ringing quality, like a gong being struck in echo to the vowels. "You don't speak mine?"

"I haven't got the range," replied Jed. They stood looking at each other with curiosity, but without emotion, like professional antagonists.

"So," said the Pellie. "It takes a trained voice, you." He was referring to the tonal changes in the language of his race, which covers several octaves, even for the expression of simple ideas. "Why you have called?"

"We were wondering," said Jed, "how you thought you could take our ship and carry it through the warfleet we're due to pass in five hours."

"You stay in ship, you," answered the other, "when we pass by fleet we let you leave ship by small boat."

"I bet," said Jed.

The Pleiadan did not shrug, but the tone of his voice conveyed the sense of it. "Your choice, you."

"I'll make you a deal," said Jed. "Let us out into the lifeboats now. None of us can turn at this velocity, so we'll all ride together up as far as the base. Once our small boats are safe under the guns of the fleet, you can chase the ship here and take it over without any trouble."

"Only-one person you leave on ship blows it up," said the Pleiadan. "No. You stay. Say nothing to fleetships. We stay close in for one pip on screen Arcturus. After we pass, we let you go. You trust us."

"Well," said Jed. "You can't blame a man for trying." He waved to the Pellie, who repeated the gesture and cut the connection. "That's that," Jed went on, turning back to the other two humans, as Tommy thoughtfully returned the star-picture to the screen. The occulting shape that was the ship they had just been talking to was looming quite large now, indicating its closeness.

"D'you think there's any chance of him doing what he says?" Barney asked the Captain.

"No reason to, and plenty of reason not to," replied Jed. "That way he keeps the two lifeboats with the ship—they're valuable in their own right." This was true, as all three men knew. A lifeboat was nothing less than a spaceship in miniature—as long as you kept it away from large planetary bodies, whose gravity were too much for the simple, one-way-thrust engines.

"I suppose the passengers will have to be told," broke in Tommy. "They'll be seeing it on the lounge screen sooner or later. What do you say, Jed?"

"Let's not borrow trouble until we have to," frowned the captain. They were all thinking the same thing, imagining the passenger's reactions to an announcement of the true facts of the situation. Hysteria is a nasty thing for a man to witness just before his own death.

"I wish there was something the fleet could do," said Tommy a trifle wistfully. He knew the hopelessness of the situation as well as the two older men; but the youngness of him protested at such an early end to his life.

"If we blew ourselves up, they'd get *him*, eh, Jed?" said Barney.

"No doubt of it," said the captain. "But I can't with these passengers. If it was us . . ."

There was the sudden suck of air, and the muted slam of the opening and closing of the bulkhead door between the control section and the passengers lounge above. Leni Hargen, the chief steward swung, down the ladder, agile in spite of his ninety years, his small, wiry figure topped by a face like an ancient monkey's. He joined the circle.

"Got company have we, Jed?" he asked, his sharp voice echoing off the metal, equipment-jammed walls.

"A Pellie," Jed nodded. "The pay-load excited?"

"So-so," replied Leni. "It hasn't struck home yet. First thing they think of when they see another ship is that it's human, of course. 'Damned clever, these aliens, but you don't mean to say they can really do what we do' —that sort of attitude. No, they think it's human. And they want to know who their traveling companions are; sent me up to ask."

"I'll go talk to them," said Jed.

"Why talk?" said Leni. Living closest of them all to the passengers, he had the most contempt for them. "Won't do no good. Wait till the long-nose gets close, then touch off the fuel, and let everybody die happy."

Barney swore. "He's right, Jed. We don't have a prayer, none of us. And I want to go when the old girl goes."

He was talking about the *Teakettle*, and the captain winced. With the exception of Tommy and the assistant steward, the ship had been their life for over half a century. It was unthinkable to imagine an existence without her. The thought of Tommy made him glance at the young mate. "What d'you say, son?"

"I . . ." Tommy hesitated. Life was desperately important to him and at the same time he was afraid of sounding like a coward. "I'd like to wait," he said at last, shamefacedly.

"I'm glad to hear it," replied Jed, decisively. "Because that's what we're going to do. I know what you think of your charges, Leni; but so far as I'm concerned, human life rates over any ship—including this one. And as long as there's one wild chance to take, I've got to take it."

"What chance?" said Leni. "They promise to turn us loose?"

Jed nodded. "They did. And I'm going to have to go on the assumption that they will."

"They will like . . ."

"Steward!" said Jed; and Leni shut his mouth. "I'll go out and talk to the passengers. The rest of you wait here."

He turned and went up the ladder toward the lounge door in the face of their silence.

The hydraulically-operated door whooshed away from its air seal as he turned the handle, and sucked back into position after he had stepped through. He stood on the upper level of the lounge, looking down its length at the gay swirl of colorfully dressed passengers. For a moment he stood unnoticed, seeing the lounge as it had been in the days when it was the main hold and he was younger. Then "Oh, there's the captain!" cried someone; and they flocked around him, chattering questions. He held up his hand for silence.

"I have a very serious announcement to make," he said. "The ship you see pulling up on us is not human but Pleiadan. They are not particularly interested in humans, but they want this ship. So after we pass Arcturus Station, we may have to take to the lifeboats and abandon the ship to them—unless some other means of dealing with the situation occurs."

He stopped and waited, bracing himself for what

he knew would follow:—first the stunned silence; then the buzz of horrified talk amongst themselves; and finally the returning to him of their attention and their questions.

"Are you sure, Captain?"

"Look for yourself," Jed waved a hand at the screen at the far end of the lounge on which the ship was now quite noticeable. "And I've talked to their captain."

"What did he say?" they cried, a dozen voices at once.

"He gave me the terms I just passed on to you," said Jed.

A silence fell on them. Looking down into their faces, Jed read their expressions clearly. This threat was too fantastic; there must be someone who had blundered. The spaceship company? The captain?

They looked back up at him, and questions came fast.

"Why don't we speed up and run away from them?"

Patiently Jed explained that maximum acceleration for humans was no more than the maximum acceleration for Pellies; and that the "speed" of a ship depended on the length of time it had been undergoing acceleration.

"Can't we dodge them?"

A little cruelly, Jed described what even a fraction of a degree of sudden alteration of course would do to the people within the ship at this present velocity.

"The warships!" someone was clamoring, an elderly, professional looking man. "You can call them, Captain!"

"If they came to meet us," said Jed, "we'd pass at such relatively high velocities that they could do us no good. We can only continue on our present course, decelerating as we normally would, and hope to get safely away from the ship after we pass Arcturus station."

The mood of the crowd in the lounge began to change. Stark fear began to creep in, and an ugly note ran through it.

"It's up to you," said one woman, her face whitened

and sharply harsh with unaccustomed desperation. "You do something!"

"Rest assured," Jed answered her, speaking to them all. "Whatever I and the crew can do, will be done. Meanwhile . . ." he caught the eye of Eli Pellew, the young assistant steward, standing at the back of the room. "The bar will be closed; and I'll expect all of you to remain as quiet as possible. Pellew, come up forward when you've closed the bar. That's all ladies and gentlemen."

He turned and went back through the door, the babble of voices behind him shut off suddenly by its closing. He re-descended the ladder to find the mate, engineer and steward in deep discussion, which broke off as he came in.

"What's this?" he said cheerfully. "Mutiny?"

"Council of war," said Barney. "It's your decision, but we thought . . ."

"Go ahead," said Jed. Sixty years of experience had taught him when to stand on his rights as captain, and when to fit in as one of the group.

"We've been talking a few things over," said Barney, "proceeding on the assumption—which most of us figure is a downright fact—that the Pellie hasn't any intention of letting us go, anyway."

"Go on."

"Well," said Barney. Almost exactly Jed's age and almost his equal in rank, the engineer slipped easily into the position of spokesman for the rest of the crew. "Following that line of thought, the conclusion is we've got nothing to lose. So to start out with, why not notify the Arcturus Base ships, anyway?"

"Because he just *might* keep that promise," said Jed. Behind them, the lounge door swished and banged. Pellew came down the steps, his collar and stewards jacket somewhat messed up.

"They're steaming up in there," he announced.

"Better go back and dog that door shut then," said Jed.

"I already did," replied Eli, his round young face

under its blond hair rosy with excitement. "I locked the connecting door to the galley, too. They're shut in."

"Good job," approved Jed. "Hope it doesn't lead to panic, though. I may have to talk to them again. You were saying, Barney . . ."

"The point is," said the engineer, taking up his argument again, "we're like a walnut in its shell with the difference that they want the shell, not the meat inside it. The way to take a ship like this is with a boarding party cutting its way through the main lock. Bloody, but the least damaging to the ship, itself. They won't want to fire on us; and if they try to put a boarding party aboard between here and Arcturus Base, we'll certainly message ahead and the warships'll have no reason for not opening fire on them. *But* if we simply message ahead and stay put, they'll just have to ride along and hope to use us for hostages when we reach the Base area."

"Sensible," said Jed, "provided they really don't mean to let us get away afterward."

"You know they don't, Jed," protested the engineer. "When did they ever let crew or passengers get away? It's not in their psychology—*I* think."

"They like to tidy up afterward, that's true," said Jed. He thought for a minute. "All right; we'll call. *Then* what do you suggest?"

There was a moment's uncomfortable silence.

"At least we know *he* won't get away then," said old Leni. "The warships'll follow and take care of him."

Jed smiled a little sadly. "I thought as much." He glanced at Tommy. "Well, make a message off. How long should it take to reach the Base?"

"About ten minutes."

"All right," Jed nodded. "Let me know if you rouse any reaction from our friend behind us." He looked at the stewards. "You two keep an eye on the passengers; Barney, come along with me."

They had been shipmates and friends for a long time. Barney turned and followed without a word as the captain took the three steps of the down ladder to the bulkhead door leading under the passenger quarters; and led the way through.

They stepped into a narrow passageway that was all metal, except for the rubbery plastic matting underfoot; the door sucked to behind them. Like all sections of the ship sealed by the heavy doors, it was soundproof to all other sections. But the light overhead was merely an occasional glimmer from spaced tubes; and the passageway itself was so narrow that there was barely room for two men to stand breast-to-breast and talk.

Jed, therefore, did not talk here. Instead he led the way back down the ship, ducking at the middle where the lifeboat blisters—one on each side of the ship— bulged down into the passage; and up three more steps at the far end. Here another door waited to be passed; when they had gone through it, they found themselves in the central tube that connected the payload section of the ship with the drive section where the atomics were located.

This passage was wider, being the full size of the tube, and its circular shape apparent to the eye. Two and a half meters in diameter was the tube, but its walls were relatively thin and uninsulated—except for a radiation protective coating between the two skins of metal that made the tube. In spite of the ships heating system, the ''cold of space'' seemed to seep through. Jed led the way to the midpoint of the tube where two small vision screens were set, one on each side of the tube. These relayed the picture—seen by antennae arms that extended like two huge knitting needles jutting out on each side of the ship beyond the screens—and looked back to scan each its own side of the space-going vessel. The trouble-shooting screens. Jed gestured at them, to the identical dumbbell shape imaged on each.

''What do you see, Barney?''

The engineer looked at the screens and back at his captain, puzzled. ''The ship,'' he said at last. ''Why, what do you see?''

"A fifty-fifty chance."

At that moment, there was a sudden shock that shook the vessel from end to end and sent the two men staggering. Recovering first, the captain took two quick steps back to the screen. On the rear left could now be seen, beyond the bulge of the drive section, the distant forward half of the Pleiadan ship. On the drive section itself was a black hole with outcurling ragged metal edges—the mark of a hit by an explosive shell in space.

"So they don't want to fire on us," said Jed, turning to Barney grimly.

The engineer looked shaken. "The message to Arcturus Base must have made him mad." Suddenly he turned and began plunging back down the tunnel. "I've got to find out what damage they did!" he shouted back.

Jed nodded; turning on his heel, he hurried back toward the control room. He came up the ladder to find the young first mate and Leni facing each other. Tommy was white, but the eyes of the wizened little steward glowed black with rage.

"Ram them!" shouted the small man, spinning on Jed as he came up the three steps of the ladder in one jump.

"Leni," said Jed, coldly. "You're under arrest; get to your quarters and stay there."

The steward hesitated, his old face twisted and violent. Suddenly, the expression of his features twisted and broke, leaving him looking simply ancient and pathetic. He choked on a sob and turned away, stumbling blindly toward the door on the level of the cabin floor, between the two stairways, that led to the captains and crew quarters under the upper level of the passenger lounge.

"Go with him," Jed instructed Eli Pellew, who was still at his station by the intercom screen, watching proceedings among the passengers. "Wait a second," he added, as the young second steward turned to go. "How've they been in there?"

"Noisy, but quiet now," answered the boy. "That

81

shot we took seems to have quieted them. They're praying, some of them.''

Jed nodded, and Eli dived through the door leading back to crew's quarters. The captain turned back to Tommy. ''Have you touched anything since we were fired on?''

''No sir,'' said Tommy. ''I had my hands full, keeping Leni off the controls. But we're tumbling end-over-end.''

''Good. We won't touch anything. Make him wonder whether he did us any vital damage, or not. Any answer from Arcturus?''

''Just before you came back,'' answered the mate. ''They acknowledged and said they were standing by to receive or follow us.''

''Also good. I've got a gamble in mind; but it's among the three of us—you, Barney, and me; and he's back looking at the drive section. There's nothing more to be done here. I don't want to answer the Pellie if he calls us, anyway; keep him guessing. Come on with me back and we'll talk with Barney.''

A curious look in the younger man's eyes warned Jed he was talking with an unusual excitement. Mentally reproving himself, he turned on his heel and led the way back down below the passenger section and through the full length of the tube back to the drive section. They stepped through a further door into one vast chamber honeycombed with equipment and to be traversed only by a network of ladders and catwalks.

''Barney!'' Jed yelled.

''Yo!'' came a distant answer and shortly the engineer came into view whisking his heavy old bulk up and down ladders with the agility of long practice. He came forward at a level about two meters over their head and dropped hand over hand down a ladder to stand at last in front of them.

''How was it?'' asked the captain.

''Not bad, thank the Lord,'' said Barney, wiping his face. There was a black smudge of resealing material on his forehead. "It was back of the fuel bins and the whole section sealed off automatically."

"Barney . . ." said Jed.

"Yes?" The engineer had found a cleaner-cloth in his pocket and was scrubbing at the black gunk below his receded hairline.

"You remember we were looking at the ship and I said I thought I saw a fifty-fifty chance?"

"That's right." The hand holding the cloth dropped suddenly to Barney's side and he looked at his captain with alert interest.

"Well, tell me something," said Jed. "We haven't used power since before the Pellie showed up. That means the tubes have all been closed, haven't they?"

"Of course," said the engineer, indignantly. "They're always closed immediately after firing; you know that."

"And with the tubes closed, our back end looks just like our front, doesn't it?"

"Why, sure," said Barney, "but I still don't see what good that does us."

"When we're all in one piece, it doesn't," replied Jed. "But suppose, just as we hit the Arcturus Base area, we break in the middle of the connecting tube and our two halves go in opposite directions? What's the Pellie to do then? He can run down one section only at the cost of getting separated from the other; and by that time the warships'll be up. So if we cut the ship in half, it gives us an even chance of being the section he doesn't chase."

His words left the two other men in a stunned silence for several seconds. Tommy was the first to recover. His eyes lit up at the possibility and he wheeled on the engineer. "That's terrific—isn't it Barney? We can fool him! Isn't that a fine idea?"

To the younger man's surprise, the engineer did not take fire from his enthusiasm. In fact, he pursed his heavy lips, doubtfully. "I don't know," he said slowly. "We'd have to think it over."

Jed was watching his old friend and shipmate with hard, bright eyes. "All right, cut it out, Barney."

The engineer raised innocent, wondering eyes to the captain. "Cut it out?" he echoed. "I don't know what you mean, Jed."

"You know damn well what I mean," said Jed. "I already had to put Leni under arrest in his quarters, with Eli as guard over him, because of the same attitude you're taking. She's a fine old ship, Barney and I love her, too—more than anything else I can think of. But get this straight. The passenger's lives come first and ours too. Then the *Teakettle. Is that clear?*"

The last three words came out like the crack of a whip. Barney dropped his head, and Tommy was astonished to see the glint of tears in the old man's eyes. "I don't know what I'll do without her," he mumbled.

"Nor I," answered Jed, more gently now. "But what must be, must, Barney. We can't become selfish because our remaining years are short. Now . . . how are we going to cut the tube?"

"Explosive?" suggested Tommy. "Have we got any?"

"Not a gram," said Jed, grimly.

Barney spoke up. "There's cutting torches back in the drive section."

Jed bit his lower lip. "I don't like that notion too well," he said, slowly. "It means we'd have to work in suits, because we'd loose air from the tube with the first hole made. And then, they'd see us busy at it and have time to think of some counter-move."

"The metal's thin," said Tommy. "If we pried off the inside plates with a crowbar, and chiseled out the insulation, a metal saw should do the work."

"Fine," said Barney. "Only we don't have a metal saw."

"I thought every drive section had metal saws among its tools," Tommy said.

"Do you think I carry a machine ship? Torches were all I ever needed."

The old man was still upset. Jed, who had been thinking, spoke up. "We've got signal flares, haven't we, Tom?"

"Yes sir," answered Tommy. The emergency equipment was his responsibility.

"Isn't the powder in them hot enough to melt through the outer skin of the tube here?"

"By God, yes," said Tommy. "It's got a thermite base; this stuff'd boil like water."

"Then that's it," said Jed. "Go bring us as much as you've got." Tommy started off at a run down the tube.

Jed turned to the engineer, who was leaning, his face sagging, against the curve of the wall. "Don't take it so hard, you old idiot!" he said, in a fierce, soft voice. "Chances are the Pellie'll give up when he sees us split. Then it's just a matter of running the two halves down and sticking them together again."

Barney pushed himself away from the wall and shook his head. "We'll kill her; you know we will. We'll kill her." And he turned and moved heavily off in the direction of the drive section, passing through the door and leaving Jed alone.

The young mate seemed to take a long time returning and Jed had the chance to feel his age and the loneliness that was to come; before the payload-section door opened and Tommy backed through, pushing his way with his shoulders, his arms loaded down with the long metal tubes of the flares.

"Stack them here," said Jed, taking charge. "Now, how are we going to stick the powder to the wall?"

". . . Thought of everything," grunted Tommy. He settled his armload on the floor, and, reaching around behind him, unhooked two short crowbars from his belt. His bulging pockets produced several bottles of the pitch-like emergency sealer. "We pry off the inner skin, gouge out insulation to the outer skin, and seal the powder in with gunk."

"Good boy," approved Jed.

They set to work, captain and mate together. In the narrow space of the tube, back-to-back, they grunted and pried until a half-meter width of the inner metal panelling had been removed. Then the sharp points of the crowbars came into action; they chipped and pounded at the heavy, brittle insulation until metal showed through beyond. A fine, searing dust rose from the fragmented insulation and hung in the passage. They coughed and choked but worked on.

"All done," said Tommy, finally. "Except for the control cables." He was referring to the thick metal conduits running between the control room and the drive section.

"Leave them—they'll burn, too," wheezed Jed. "Now help me with the powder."

Step by step they drew their circle around the tube; white, innocent-looking powder, held in by sticky blackness. Finally, they were done.

"Fuse?" said Jed.

"Here." Tommy pulled a coil of shining, slim wire from within his tunic. It was regulation electrical contact cable, spliced and fitted with an explosive cap. Jed took the end and wedged it into the gunk, pushing it through to the powder beneath. Then they moved back, paying it out as they went, along the tube, through the door, up the under passage and into the control room.

The two men collapsed on to seats before the equipment boards.

"Whew!" said Tommy, after a few moments. "That was a job!"

Jed nodded. He was feeling his age, and there was a sharp pain in his chest. After he had rested a few more minutes, he got up and began checking their position.

They were close to Arcturus Base Area, that imaginary globe of space which enclosed the waiting warfleet, whose duty is to guard the Arcturian planets. Jed set his viewer up to maximum range and probed the empty distances ahead. There was nothing on it, but the armed ships which might rescue them could not be too far away.

"I'll give them another fifteen minutes; then we'll split," said Jed, glancing at the younger man. Suddenly he was aware of the emptiness of the control room. "By heaven, Barney's still back in the drive section. Get him up front here!"

Tommy dived for the down stairs; and vanished through the door. Jed grimaced and glanced at the clock. He reached out to call ahead to the armed vessels, then remembered the shot that had been fired at them on the previous occasion and took his hand away. He checked the scanner.

There were a couple of pips tiny in the distance, too far to show on the screen.

The waiting seemed interminable. Finally Tommy reappeared, almost literally herding the old engineer before him.

"We aren't going to waste any more time," said Jed. "Take seats and strap yourself in." He leaned over and keyed in the intercom to the passenger lounge.

"Attention," he said. The view on the screen faded from the stars to the lounge's interior. Weary, hopeless and frightened people looked up at him without much reaction. "Will you please take seats and fasten yourself in them. We are about to attempt evasive action."

"What for?" said a tall man, standing greyfaced toward the back of the room. "You said before it was no use."

"We're almost up to the Arcturus Base Fleet," answered Jed. "It may do some good now. Will you strap yourself in, please?"

"Why should we strap ourselves in?" cried a little man who had been sitting with his head in his hands. He now raised it, his deep eyes wild. "Why did you lock the doors? What . . ."

"Strap yourselves in! That's an order!" thundered Jed suddenly, tried beyond all patience.

Stunned by the volume of the intercom amplifier, the passengers fell into their seats without further protest, stumbling over each other in their haste. Safety belts snapped; and when Jed could tell by looking at the screen that all were secured, he switched back to an outside view.

Ahead, the warships of the Base were being rapidly overhauled in spite of the fact that they were building up velocity in the same direction as the *Teakettle* and the Pleiadan at maximum bearable acceleration. The alien ship itself was hanging in close and directly behind the *Teakettle*, so that they too would show as long as possible as a single pip on the warship's screens. Now was the time to do whatever could be done.

Jed turned and threw a quick glance about the control room. Leni and young Eli Pellew had come out of the crew quarters and were strapped in side by side, in the observer seats. Tommy must have warned them. The young mate himself was strapped into the acceleration chair before the auxiliary screen; and on Jed's other side to his right, Barney sat belted to the chair before the direct drive controls. This was his proper post; and although there was nothing now for him to do there, Jed thought he understood the impulse that had pushed the old man to his accustomed place. Jed reached for the contact switch and lifted it. The cable trailed away from him on the floor, silver to the bottom of the door and disappeared beneath it.

Jed glanced once more about the control room. Tommy's face, to his left, was tense on the screen, watching the growing shapes of the warships, pale—but not so pale as the face of Eli Pellew behind him, who seemed drugged with shock. Beside Eli's young face, Leni's eyes glared up at him, black and bitter. On his right, Barney sat slumped before his board, his fingers resting laxly upon the controls, his face unreadable.

He seemed chained and bound to inertness by the depression within him. But as Jed turned his way and closed his fingers about the switch, from the corner of his eyes, he seemed to see the fingers of the old man flicker, once.

And almost in the same heartbeat, closed his own fingers, closing the switch.

The ship bucked once like an insane thing as the super-heated air in the tube exploded outward through the vaporized metal of the outer skin. The stars spun like a pinwheel on the screen; and into view swam the full length of the Pleiadan and the tumbling other half of the *Teakettle*. Fingers working on the direction finders, flickering but working on the self-contained emergency power stored in the control room itself, Jed kept the two images on the screen together.

As the warships swelled on the screen, the nose of the Pellie ship swung first in this direction, then in that, sniffing after the two fragments of what had been the *Teakettle*, like a hunting terrier after two scuttling mice. The warships were growing fast, and for the alien, death was certain. It fired once at the drive section; then, ominously, its nose swung toward the payload half. Nose-on on the screen it stood before them.

"Sweetheart . . ." whispered Barney. And at that moment, from the tattered half-tube attached to the fleeing drive section shot a sudden, long spurt of yellow flame, hurtling it further and faster . . .

. . . And the alien swung to follow it. For the first time, from its tubes came a flare of power—not a change of direction, but an additional thrust forward that, though diverging, brought it up level and close to the burning tube and ball.

And its guns began to pound the fleeing drive section.

Behind Jed, Leni sobbed once. And Jed, looking over at Barney, saw the heavy old man press back in his seat, eyes wide, but with an incomprehensible wildness on his face.

The warships were closing up now. Ranging shells from their heavy guns began to search out the alien. But before they could strike home Barney shouted like a berserker, his old voice cracking. The drive section opened up like a flower into a brilliant pure white blossom of flame whose lightest touch was extinction. And the alien ship flared like a burnt moth.

In the silence of the control room they sat and watched it burn. And when the fire had died; and the warships were far behind, but coming up fast now, Jed turned to the engineer, "Thanks, Barney," he said.

"Thank her," said Barney emptily. "All I did was to pull the damping rods."

They looked at each other across the little distance and the useless controls between; two old men understanding each other.

Jed turned away and flicked on the intercom. "Attention all passengers," he said. "You may unstrap now."

An Ounce of Emotion

I

"Well? Are the ships joined—or not?" demanded
Arthur Mial.

"Look for yourself!" said Tyrone Ross.

Mial turned and went on out of the room. All right,
thought Ty savagely, call it a personality conflict. Putting
a tag on it is one thing, doing something about it another.
And I have to do something—it could just be the fuse to
this nitro-jelly situation he, I, and Annie are all sitting on.
There must be some way I can break down this feeling
between us.

Ty glanced for a moment across the spaceliner stateroom at the statistical analysis instrument, called Annie,
now sitting silent and unimpressive as a black steamer
trunk against a far wall.

It was Annie who held the hope of peace for thousands of cubic light years of interstellar space in every
direction. Annie—with the help of Ty. And the dubious
help of Mial. The instrument, thought Ty grimly, deserved
better than the two particular human companions the Laburti
had permitted, to bring her to them.

He turned back to the vision screen he had been watching earlier.

On it, pictured from the viewpoint of one of the tractor mechs now maneuvering the ship, this leviathan of a Laburti spaceliner he was on was being laid alongside and only fifty yards from an equally huge Chedal vessel. Even Ty's untrained eye could see the hair-trigger risks in bringing those hundreds of thousands of tons of mass so close together. But with the two Great Races, so-called, poised on the verge of conflict, the Chedal Observer of the Annie Demonstration five days from now could not be simply ferried from his ship to this like any ordinary passenger.

The two ships must be faced, main airlock to main airlock, and a passageway fitted between the locks. So that the Chedal and his staff could stroll aboard with all due protocol. Better damage either or both of the giant craft than chance any suspicion of a slight by one of the Great Races to a representative of the other.

For the Laburti and the Chedal were at a sparking point. A sparking point of war that—but of course neither race of aliens was concerned about that—could see small Earth drafted into the armed camp of its huge Laburti neighbor; and destroyed by the Chedal horde, if the inter-stellar conflict swept past Alpha Centauri.

It was merely, if murderously, ironic in this situation that Ty and Mial who came bearing the slim hope of peace that was Annie, should be themselves at a sparking point. A sparking point willed by neither—but to which they had both been born.

Ty's thoughts came back from the vision screen to their original preoccupation.

It happened sometimes, he thought. It just—happened. Sometimes, for no discernable reason, suddenly and with-out warning, two men meeting for the first time felt the ancient furies buried deep in their forebrains leap abruptly and readily to life. It was rapport between individuals turned inside out—anti-rapport. Under it, the animal instinct in each man instantly snarled and bristled, recognizing a mortal enemy—an enemy not in act or attitude, but simply in *being*.

So it had happened with Ty—and Mial. Back on Earth, thought Ty now, while there was still a chance to do something about the situation, they had each been too civilized to speak up about it. Now it was too late. The mistake was made.

And mistake it had been. For, practical engineer and reasonable man that Ty was, reasonable man and practical politician that Mial was, to the rest of mankind— to each other they were tigers. And common sense dictated that you did not pen two tigers alone together for two weeks; for a delicate mission on which the future existence of the human race might depend. Already, after nine days out—

"We'll have to go meet the Chedal." It was Mial, reentering the room. Ty turned reflexively to face him.

The other man was scarcely a dozen years older than Ty; and in many ways they were nearly alike. There could not be half an inch or five pounds of weight difference between them, thought Ty. Like Ty, Mial was square-shouldered and leanly built. But his hair was dark where Ty's was blond; and that dark hair had started to recede. The face below it was handsome, rather than big-boned and open like Ty's. Mial, at thirty-six, was something of a wonder boy in politics back on Earth. Barely old enough for the senatorial seat he held, he had the respect of almost everyone. But he had been legal counsel for some unsavory groups in the beginning of his career. He would know how, thought Ty watching him now, to fight dirty if he had to. And the two of them were off with none but aliens to witness.

"I know," said Ty now, harshly. He turned to follow Mial as the other man started out of the room. "What about Annie?"

Mial looked back over his shoulder.

"She's safe enough. What good's a machine to them if no one but a human can run her?" Mial's voice was almost taunting. "You can't go up with the big boys, Ross, and act scared."

Ty's face flushed with internal heat—but it was true, what Mial had said. A midget trying to make peace with giants did well not to act doubtful or afraid. Mial had courage to see it. Ty felt an unwilling touch of admiration for the man. I could almost like him for that, he thought—if I didn't hate his guts.

By the time they got to the air-lock, the slim, dog-faced, and darkly-robed Laburti were in their receiving line, and the first of the squat, yellow-furred Chedal forms were coming through. First came the guards; then the Observer himself, distinguishable to a human eye only by the sky-blue harness he wore. The tall, thin form of the robed Laburti Captain glided forward to welcome him aboard first; and then the Observer moved down the line, to confront Mial.

A high-pitched chattering came from the Chedal's lipless slit of a mouth, almost instantly overridden by the artificial, translated human speech from the black translator collar around the alien's thick, yellow-furred neck. Shortly, Mial was replying in kind, his own black translator collar turning his human words into Chedal chitterings. Ty stood listening, half-selfconscious, half-bored.

"—and my Demonstration Operator." Ty woke suddenly to the fact that Mial was introducing him to the Chedal.

"Honored," said Ty, and heard his collar translating.

"May I invite you both to my suite now, immediately, for the purpose of improving our acquaintance . . ." The invitation extended itself, became flowery, and ended with a flourish.

"It's an honor to accept . . ." Mial was answering. Ty braced himself for at least another hour of this before they could get back to their own suite.

Then his breath caught in his throat.

". . . for myself, that is," Mial was completing his answer. "Unfortunately, I earlier ordered my Operator to return immediately to his device, once these greetings were over. And I make it a practice never to change an order. I'm sure you understand."

"Of course. Some other time I will host your Operator. Shall we two go?" The Chedal turned and led off. Mial was turning with him, when Ty stepped in front of him.

"Hold on—" Ty remembered to turn off his translator collar. "What's this about your *ordering* me—"

Mial flicked off his own translator collar.

"You heard me," he said. He stepped around Ty and walked off. Ty stood, staring after him. Then, conscious of the gazing Laburti all about him, he turned and headed back toward their own suite.

Once back there, and with the door to the ship's corridor safely closed behind him, he swore and turned to checking out Annie, to make sure there had been no investigation or tampering with her innards while he was absent. Taking off the side panel of her case, he pinched his finger between the panel and the case and swore again. Then he sat down suddenly, ignoring Annie and began to think.

II

With the jab of pain from the pinched finger, an incredible suspicion had sprung, full-armed into his brain. For the first time he found himself wondering if Mial's lie to the Chedal about an 'order' to Ty had been part of some plan by the other man against Ty. A plan that required Mial's talking with the Chedal Observer alone, before Ty did.

It was, Ty had to admit, the kind of suspicion that only someone who felt as he did about Mial could have dreamed up. And yet . . .

The orders putting the Annie Demonstration Mission— which meant Annie and Ty—under the authority of Mial had been merely a polite fiction. A matter of matching the high rank and authority of the Laburti and Chedal officials who would be watching the Demonstration as Observers.

Ty had been clearly given to understand that by his own Department chief, back on Earth.

In other words, Mial had just now stopped playing according to the unwritten rules of the Mission. That might bode ill for Ty. And, thought Ty now, suddenly, it might bode even worse for the success of the Mission. But it was unthinkable that Mial would go so far as to risk that.

For, it was one thing to stand here with Annie and know she represented something possessed by neither the Laburti nor the Chedal technologies. It was all right to remind oneself that human science was growing like the human population; and that population was multiplying at close to three per cent per year—as opposed to a fraction of a per cent for the older Chedal and Laburti populations.

But there were present actualities that still had to be faced—like the size of this ship, and that of the Chedal ship now parting from it. Also, like the twenty-odd teeming worlds apiece, the thousands of years each of post-atomic civilization, the armed might either sprawling alien empire could boast.

Mial could not—would not—be playing some personal game in the face of all this. Ty shook his head angrily at the thought. No man could be such a fool, no matter what basic emotional factor was driving him.

When Mial returned to their stateroom suite a couple of hours later, Ty made an effort to speak pleasantly to him.

"Well?" said Ty, "how'd it go? And when am I to meet him?"

Mial looked at him coldly.

"You'll be told," he said, and went on into his bedroom.

But, in the four days left of the trip to the Laburti World, where the Demonstration was to be given before a joint audience of Laburti and Chedal Observers, it became increasingly apparent Ty was not to meet the Chedal. Meanwhile, Mial was increasingly in conference with the alien representative.

Ty gritted his teeth. At least, at their destination the Mission would be moving directly to the Human Consulate. And the Consul in charge was not a human, but a Laburti citizen who had contracted for the job of representing the Earth race. Mial could hardly hold secret conferences with the Chedal under a Laburti nose.

Ty was still reminding himself of this as the spaceliner finally settled toward their destination—a fantastic metropolis, with eight and ten thousand foot tall buildings rising out of what Ty had been informed was a quarter-mile depth of open ocean. Ty had just finished getting Annie rigged for handling when Mial came into the room.

"Ready?" demanded Mial.

"Ready," said Ty.

"You go ahead with Annie and the baggage—" The sudden, soft hooting of the landing horn interrupted Mial, and there was a faint tremor all through the huge ship as it came to rest in its landing cradle of magnetic forces; the main door to the suite from the corridor swung open. A freight-handling mech slid into the room and approached Annie.

"I'll meet you outside in the taxi area," concluded Mial.

Ty felt abrupt and unreasonable suspicion.

"Why?" he asked sharply.

Mial had already turned toward the open door through which the mech had just entered. He paused and turned back to face Ty; a smile, razor blade thin and cruel altered his handsome face.

"Because that's what I'm going to do," he said softly, and turned again toward the door.

Ty stared after him for a moment, jarred and irresolute at the sudden, fresh outbreak of hostilities, and Mial went out through the door.

"Wait a minute!" snapped Ty, heading after him. But the other man was already gone, and the mech, carrying Annie and following close behind him, had blocked Ty's path. Cold with anger, Ty swung back to check their personal baggage, including their food supplies, as another mech entered to carry these to the outside of the ship.

When he finally got outside to the disembarkation area, and got the baggage, as well as Annie, loaded on to one of the flying cargo platforms that did taxi service among the Laburti, he looked around for Mial. He discovered the other man a short distance away in the disembarkation area, talking again with a blue-harnessed, yellow-furred form.

Grimly, Ty turned on his translator collar and gave the cargo platform the address of the human Consulate. Then, he lifted a section of the transparent cover of the platform and stepped aboard, to sit down on the luggage and wait for Mial. After a while, he saw Mial break off his conversation and approach the cargo platform. The statesman spoke briefly to the cargo platform, something Ty could not hear from under the transparent cover, then came aboard and sat down next to Ty.

The platform lifted into the air and headed in between the blue and gray metal of the towers with their gossamer connecting bridges.

"I already told it where to take us," said Ty.

Mial turned to look at him briefly and almost contemptuously, then turned away again without answering.

The platform slid amongst the looming towers and finally flew them in through a wide window-opening, into a room set up with human-style furniture. They got off, and Ty looked around as the platform began to unload the baggage. There was no sign of the Laburti individual who filled the role of human Consul. Sudden suspicion blossomed again in Ty.

"Wait a minute—" He wheeled about—but the platform, already unloaded, was lifting out through the window opening again. Ty turned on Mial. "This isn't the Consulate!"

"That's right," Mial almost drawled the words. "It's a hotel—the way they have them here. The Chedal Observer recommended it to me."

"Recommended—?" Ty stared. "We're supposed to go to the Consulate. You can't—"

"Can't I?" Mial's eyes were beginning to blaze. The throttled fury in him was yammering to be released, evidently, as much as its counterpart in Ty. "I don't trust that Consulate, with its Laburti playing human Consul. Here, if the Chedal wants to drop by—"

"He's not supposed to drop by!" Ty snarled. "We're here to demonstrate Annie, not gabble with the Observers. What'll the Laburti think if they find you and the Chedal glued together half of the time?" He got himself under control and said in a lower voice. "We're going back to the Consulate, now—"

"Are we?" Mial almost hissed. "Are you forgetting that the orders show *me* in charge of this Demonstration— and that the aliens'll believe those orders? Besides, you don't know your way around here. And, after talking to the Chedal—I do!"

He turned abruptly and strode over to an apparently blank wall. He rapped on it, and flicked on his translator collar and spoke to the wall.

"Open up!" The wall slid open to reveal what was evidently an elevator tube. He stepped into it and turned to smile mockingly at Ty, drifting down out of sight. The wall closed behind him.

"Open up!" raged Ty, striding to the wall and rapping on it. He flicked on his translator collar. "Open up. Do you hear me? Open up!"

But the wall did not open. Ty, his knuckles getting sore, at last gave up and turned back to Annie.

III

Whatever else might be going on, his responsibility to her and the Demonstration tomorrow, remained unchanged. He got her handling rigging off, and ran a sample problem through her. When he was done, he checked the resultant figures against the answers to the problem already established by multiple statistics back on Earth. He was within a fraction of a per cent all the way down the line.

Ty glowed, in spite of himself. Operating Annie successfully was not so much a skill, as an art. In any problem, there were from fourteen to twenty factors whose values had to be adjusted according to the instincts and creativity of the Operator. It was this fact that was the human ace in the hole in this situation. Aliens could not run Annie—they had tried on Annie's prototypes and failed. Only a few specially trained and talented humans could run her successfully . . . and of these, Ty Ross was the master Operator. That was why he was here.

Now, tomorrow he would have to prove his right to that title. Under his hands Annie could show that a hundred and twenty-five Earth years after the Laburti and Chedal went to war, the winner would have a Gross Racial Product only eight per cent increased over today—so severe would the conflict have been. But in a hundred and twenty-five years of peaceful co-existence and cooperation, both races would have doubled their G.R.P.s in spite of having made only fractional increases in population. And machines like Annie, with operators like Ty, stood ready to monitor and guide the G.R.P. increases. No sane race could go to war in the face of that.

Meanwhile, Mial had not returned. Outside the weather shield of the wide window, the local sun, a G5 star, was taking its large, orange-yellow shape below the watery horizon. Ty made himself something to eat, read a while, and then took himself to bed in one of the adjoining bedrooms. But disquieting memories kept him from sleeping.

He remembered now that there had been an argument back on Earth, about the proper way to make use of Annie. He had known of this for a long time, Mial's recent actions came forcing it back into the forefront of his sleepless mind.

The political people back home had wanted Annie to be used as a tool, and a bargaining point, rather than a solution to the Laburti-Chedal confrontation, in herself. It was true, Ty reminded himself in the darkness, Mial had not been one of those so arguing. But he was of the same breed and occupation as they, reminded the little red devils of suspicion, coming out to dance on Ty's brain. With a sullen effort Ty shoved them out of his mind and forced himself to think of something else—anything else.

And, after a while, he slept.

He woke suddenly, feeling himself being shaken back to consciousness. The lights were on in the room and Mial was shaking him.

"What?" Ty sat up, knocking the other man's hand aside.

"The Chedal Observer's here with me," said Mial. "He wants a preview demonstration of the analyzer."

"A preview!" Ty burst up out of bed to stand facing the other man. "Why should he get to see Annie before the official Demonstration?"

"Because I said he could." Underneath, Mial's eyes were stained by dark half-circles of fatigue.

"Well, I say he can wait until tomorrow like the Laburti!" snapped Ty. He added, "—And don't try to pull your paper rank on me. If I don't run Annie for him, who's to do it? You?"

Mial's weary face paled with anger.

"The Chedal asked for the preview," he said, in a tight, low voice. "I didn't think I had the right to refuse him, important as this Mission is. Do you want to take the responsibility of doing it? Annie'll come up with the same answers now as seven hours from now."

"Almost the same—" muttered Ty. "They're never exact, I told you that." He swayed on his feet, caught between sleep and resentment.

"As you say," said Mial, "I can't make you do it."

Ty hesitated a second more. But his brain seemed numb.

"All right," he snapped. "I'll have to get dressed. Five minutes!"

Mial turned and went out. When Ty followed, some five minutes later, he found both the other man and the alien in the sitting room. The Chedal came toward Ty, and for a moment they were closer than they had been even in the spaceliner airlock. For the first time, Ty smelled a faint, sickening odor from the alien, a scent like overripe bananas.

The Chedal handed him a roll of paper-like material. Gibberish raved from his lipless mouth and was translated by the translator collar.

"Here is the data you will need."

"Thank you," said Ty, with bare civility. He took the roll over to Annie and examined it. It contained all the necessary statistics on both the Laburti and Chedal races, from the Gross Racial Products down to statistical particulars. He went to work, feeding the data into Annie.

Time flowed by, catching him up in the rhythm of his work as it went.

His job with Annie required just this sort of concentration and involvement, and for a little while he forgot the two watching him. He looked up at last to see the window aperture flushed with yellow-pink dawn, and guessed that perhaps an hour had gone by.

He tore loose the tape he had been handling, and walked with it to the Chedal.

"Here," he said, putting the tape into the blunt, three-fingered hands, and pointing to the first figures. "There's your G.R.P. half a standard year after agreement to co-exist with Laburti.—Up three thousands of one per cent already. And here it is at the end of a full year—"

"And the Laburti?" demanded the translated chittering of the alien.

"Down here. You see . . ." Ty talked on. The Chedal watched, his perfectly round, black eyes emotionless as the button-eyes of a child's toy. When Ty was finished, the alien, still holding the tape, swung on Mial, turning his back to Ty.

"We will check this, of course," the Chedal said to Mial. "But your price is high." He turned and went out.

Ty stood staring after him.

"What price?" he asked, huskily. His throat was suddenly dry. He swung on Mial. "What price is it that's too high?"

"The price of cooperation with the Laburti!" snarled Mial. "They and the Chedal hate each other—or haven't you noticed?" He turned and stalked off into the opposite bedroom, slamming the door behind him.

Ty stood staring at the closed surface. He made a step toward it, Mial had evidently been up all night. This, combined with the emotional situation between them, would make it pointless for Ty to try to question him.

Besides, thought Ty, hollowly and coldly, there was no need. He turned back across the room to the pile of their supplies and got out the coffeemaker. It was a little self-contained unit that could brew up a fresh cup in something like thirty seconds; for those thirty seconds, Ty kept his mind averted from the problem. Then, with the cup of hot, black coffee in his hands, he sat down to decide what to do.

Mial's answer to his question about the Chedal's mention of price had been thoughtless and transparent— the answer of a man scourged by dislike and mind-numbed by fatigue. Clearly, it could not be anything so simple as the general price of cooperation with a disliked other race, to which the Chedal Observer had been referring. No—it had to have been a specific price. And a specific price that was part of specific, personal negotations held in secret between the alien and Mial.

Such personal negotations were no part of the Demonstration plans as Ty knew them. Therefore Mial was not following those plans. Clearly he was following some other course of action.

And this, to Ty, could only be the course laid down by those political minds back on Earth who had wanted to use Annie as a pawn to their maneuvering, instead of presenting the statistical analysis instrument plainly and honestly by itself to the Laburti and the Chedal Observers.

If this was the case, the whole hope of the Demonstration hung in the balance. Mial, sparked by instinctive hatred for Ty, was opposing himself not merely to Ty but to everything Ty stood for—including the straight-forward presentation of Annie's capabilities. Instead, he must be dickering with the Chedal for some agreement that would league humanity with the Chedal and against the Laburti—a wild, unrealistic action when the solar system lay wholly within the powerful Laburti stellar sphere of influence.

A moment's annoyance on the part of the Laburti—a moment's belief that the humans had been trying to trick them and play games with their Chedal enemy—and the Laburti forces could turn Earth to a drifting cinder of a world with as little effort as a giant stepping on an ant.

If this was what Mial was doing—and by now Ty was convinced of it—the other man must be stopped, at any cost.

But how?

Ty shivered suddenly and uncontrollably. The room seemed abruptly as icy as a polar tundra.

There was only one way to stop Mial, who could not be reasoned with—by Ty, at least—either on the emotional or the intellectual level; and who held the paper proofs of authority over Ty and Annie. Mial would have to be physically removed from the Demonstration. If necessary—rather than risk the life of Earth and the whole human race—he would have to be killed.

And it would have to look like an accident. Anything else would cause the aliens to halt the Demonstration.

The shiver went away without warning—leaving only a momentary flicker of doubt in Ty, a second's wonder if perhaps his own emotional reaction to Mial was not hurrying him to take a step that might not be justified. Then, that flicker went out. With the Demonstration only hours away, Ty could not stop to examine his motives. He had to act and hope he was right.

He looked across the room at Annie. The statistical analysis instrument housed her own electrical power source and it was powerful enough to give a lethal jolt to a human heart. Her instruments and controls were insulated from the metal case, but the case itself . . .

Ty put down his coffee cup and walked over to the instrument. He got busy. It was not difficult. Half an hour later, as the sun of this world was rising out of the sea, he finished, and went back to his room for a few hours' sleep. He fell instantly into slumber and slept heavily.

IV

He jerked awake. The loon-like hooting in his ears; and standing over his bed was the darkly robed figure of a Laburti.

Ty scrambled to his feet, reaching for a bathrobe.

"What . . . ?" he blurted.

Hairless, gray-skinned and dog-faced, narrow-shouldered in the heavy, dark robes he wore, the Laburti looked back at him expressionlessly.

"Where is Demonstration Chief Arthur Mial?" The words came seemingly without emotion from the translator collar, over the sudden deep, harsh-voiced yammering from the face above it.

"I—in the bedroom."

"He is not there."

"But . . ." Ty, belting the bathrobe, strode around the alien, out of his bedroom, across the intervening room and looked into the room into which Mial had disappeared only a few hours before. The bed there was rumpled, but empty. Ty turned back into the center room where Annie stood. Behind her black metal case, the alien sun was approaching the zenith position of noon.

"You will come with me," said the Laburti.

Ty turned to protest. But two more Laburti had come into the suite, carrying the silver-tipped devices which Ty had been briefed back on Earth, were weapons. Following them came mechs which gathered up the baggage and Annie. Ty cut off the protest before it could reach his lips. There was no point in arguing. But where was Mial?

They crossed a distance of the alien city by flying

platform and came at last into another tower, and a large suite of rooms. The Laburti who had woken Ty led him into an interior room where yet another Laburti stood, robed and impassive.

"These," said the Laburti who had brought Ty there, "are the quarters belonging to me. I am the Consul for your human race on this world. This—" the alien nodded at the other robed figure, "is the Observer of our Laburti race, who was to view your device today."

The word *was*, with all the implications of its past tense, sent a chill creeping through Ty.

"Where is Demonstration Chief Arthur Mial?" demanded the Laburti Observer.

"I don't know!"

The two Laburti stood still. The silence went on in the room, and on until it began to seem to roar in Ty's ears. He swayed a little on his feet, longing to sit down, but knowing enough of protocol not to do so while the Laburti Observer was still standing. Then, finally, the Observer spoke again.

"You have been demonstrating your instrument to the Chedal," he said, "previous to the scheduled Demonstration and without consulting us."

Ty opened his mouth, then closed it again. There was nothing he could say.

The Observer turned and spoke to the Consul with his translator switched off. The Consul produced a roll of paper-like material almost identical with that the Chedal had handed Ty earlier, and passed it into Ty's hands.

"Now," said the Laburti Observer, tonelessly, "you will give a previous Demonstration to me . . ."

The Demonstration was just ending, when a distant hooting called the Laburti Consul out of the room. He returned a minute later—and with him was Mial.

"A Demonstration?" asked Mial, speaking first and looking at the Laburti Observer.

"You were not to be found," replied the alien. "And

I am informed of a Demonstration you gave the Chedal Observer some hours past.''

"Yes," said Mial. His eyes were still dark from lack of sleep, but his gaze seemed sharp enough. That gaze slid over to fasten on Ty, now. "Perhaps we'd better discuss that, before the official Demonstration. There's less than an hour left."

"You intend still to hold the original Demonstration?"

"Yes," said Mial. "Perhaps we'd better discuss that, too—alone."

"Perhaps we had better," said the Laburti. He nodded to the Consul who started out of the room. Ty stood still.

"Get going," said Mial icily to him, without bothering to turn off his translator collar. "And have the machine ready to go."

Ty turned off his own translator collar, but stood where he was. "What're you up to?" he demanded. "This isn't the way we were supposed to do things. You're running some scheme of your own. Admit it!"

Mial turned his collar off.

"All right," he said, coldly and calmly. "I've had to. There were factors you don't know anything about."

"Such as?"

"There's no time to explain now."

"I won't go until I know what kind of a deal you've been cooking up with the Chedal Observer!"

"You fool!" hissed Mial. "Can't you see this alien's listening and watching every change your face makes? I can't tell you now, and I won't tell you. But I'll tell you this—you're going to get your chance to demonstrate Annie just the way you expected to, to Chedal and Laburti together, if you go along with me. But fight me—and that chance is lost. Now, *will you go*?"

Ty hesitated a moment longer, then he turned and followed the Laburti Consul out. The alien led him to the room where Annie and their baggage had been placed, and shut him in there.

Once alone, he began to pace the floor, fury and worry boiling together inside him. Mial's last words just now had been an open ultimatum. *You're too late to stop me now*, had been the unspoken message behind those words. *Go along with me now, or else lose everything.*

Mial had been clever, He had managed to keep Ty completely in the dark. Puzzle as he would now, Ty could not figure out what it was, specifically, that Mial had set out secretly to do to the Annie Mission.

Or how much of that Mial might already have accomplished. How could Ty fight, completely ignorant of what was going on?

No, Mial was right. Ty could not refuse, blind, to do what he had been sent out to do. That way there would be no hope at all. By going along with Mial he kept alive the faint hope that things might yet, somehow, turn out as planned back on Earth. Even if—Ty paused in his pacing to smile grimly—Mial's plan included some arrangement not to Ty's personal benefit. For the sake of the original purpose of the Mission, Ty had to go through with the Demonstration, even now, just as if he was Mial's willing accomplice.

But—Ty began to pace again. There was something else to think about. It was possible to attack the problem from the other end. The accomplishment of the Mission was more important than the survival of Ty. Well, then, it was also more important than the survival of Mial— And if Mial should die, whatever commitments he had secretly made to the Chedal against the Laburti, or vice-versa, would die with him.

What would be left would be only what had been intended in the first place. The overwhelming common-sense practicality of peace in preference to war, demonstrated to both the Laburti and the Chedal.

Ty, pausing once more in his pacing to make a final decision, found his decision already made. Annie was already prepared as a lethal weapon. All he needed was to put her to use to stop Mial.

Twenty minutes later, the Laburti Consul for the human race came to collect both Ty and Annie, and bring them back to the room from which Ty had been removed, at Mial's suggestion earlier. Now, Ty saw the room held not only Mial and the Laburti Observer, but one other Laburti in addition. While across the room's width from these, were the Chedal Observer in blue harness with two other Chedals. They were all, with the exception of Mial, aliens, and their expressions were almost unreadable therefore. But, as Ty stepped into the room, he felt the animosity, like a living force, between the two groups of aliens in spite of the full room's width of distance between them.

It was in the rigidity with which both Chedal and Laburti figures stood. It was in the unwinking gaze they kept on each other. For the first time, Ty realized the need behind the emphasis on protocol and careful procedure between these two races. Here was merely a situation to which protocol was new, with a weaker race standing between representatives of the two Great Ones. But these robed, or yellow-furred, diplomats seemed ready to fly physically at each other's throats.

IV

"Get it working—" it was the voice of Mial with his translator turned off, and it betrayed a sense of the same tension in the air that Ty had recognized between the two alien groups. Ty reached for his own collar and then remembered that it was still turned off from before.

"I'll need your help," he said tonelessly. "Annie's been jarred a bit, bringing her here."

"All right," said Mial. He came quickly across the room to join Ty, now standing beside the statistical analysis instrument.

"Stand here, behind Annie," said Ty, "so you don't block my view of the front instrument panel. Reach over the case to the data sorting key here, and hold it down for me."

"This key—all right." From behind Annie, Mial's

long right arm reached easily over the top of the case, but—as Ty had planned—not without requiring the other man to lean forward and brace himself with a hand upon the top of the metal case of the instrument. A touch now by Ty on the tape control key would send upwards of thirteen thousand volts suddenly through Mial's body.

He ducked his head down and hastily began to key in data from the statistic roll lying waiting for him on a nearby table.

The work kept his face hidden, but could not halt the trembling beginning to grow inside him. His reaction against the other man was no less, but now—faced with the moment of pressing the tape control key—he found all his history and environmental training against what he was about to do. *Murder*—screamed his conscious mind—*it'll be murder!*

His throat ached and was dry as some seared and cindered landscape of Earth might one day be after the lashing of a Chedal space-based weapon. His chest muscles had tensed and it seemed hard to get his breath. With an internal gasp of panic, he realized that the longer he hesitated, the harder it would be. His finger touched and trembled against the smooth, cold surface of the tape control key, even as the fingers of his other hand continued to key in data.

"How much longer?" hissed Mial in his ear.

Ty refused to look up. He kept his face hidden. One look at that face would be enough to warn Mial.

What if you're wrong?—screamed his mind. It was a thought he could not afford to have, not with the future of the Earth and all its people riding on this moment. He swallowed, closed his eyes, and jammed sideways on the tape key with his finger. He felt it move under his touch.

He opened his eyes. There had been no sound.

He lifted his gaze and saw Mial's face only inches away staring down at him.

"What's the matter?" whispered Mial, tearingly.

Nothing had happened. Somehow Mial was still alive. Ty swallowed and got his inner trembling under control.

"Nothing . . ." he said.

"What is the cause of this conversation?" broke in the deep, yammering, translated voice of one of the Laburti. "Is there a difficulty with the device?"

"Is there?" hissed Mial.

"No . . ." Ty pulled himself together. "It'll handle it now. You can go back to them."

"All right," said Mial, abruptly straightening up and letting go of the case.

He turned and went back to join the Laburti Observer.

Ty turned back to his work and went on to produce his tape of statistical forecasts for both races. Standing in the center of the room to explain it, while the two alien groups held copies of the tape, he found his voice growing harsher as he talked.

But he made no attempt to moderate it. He had failed to stop Mial. Nothing mattered now.

These were Annie's results, he thought, and they were correct and undeniable. The two alien races could ignore them only at the cost of cutting off their noses to spite their faces. Whatever else would come from Mial's scheming and actions here—this much from Annie was unarguable. No sane race could ignore it.

When he finished, he dropped the tape brusquely on top of Annie's case and looked directly at Mial. The dark-haired man's eyes met his, unreadably.

"You'll go back and wait," said Mial, barely moving his lips. The Laburti Consul glided toward Ty. Together they left and returned to the room with the baggage, where Ty had been kept earlier.

"Your device will be here in a moment," said the Laburti, leaving him. And, in fact, a moment later a mech moved into the room, deposited Annie on the floor and withdrew. Like a man staring out of a daze, Ty fell feverishly upon the side panel of the metal case and began unscrewing the wing nuts securing it.

The panel fell away in his hands and he laid it aside. He stared into the inner workings before him, tracing the connections to the power supply, the data control key, and the case that he had made earlier. There were the wires, exactly as he had fitted them in; and there had been no lack of power evident in Annie's regular working. Now, with his forefinger half an inch above the insulation of the wires, he traced them from the data control key back to the negative power lead connection, and from the case toward its connection, with the positive power lead.

He checked, motionless, with pointing finger. The connection was made to the metal case, all right; but the other end of the wire lay limply along other connections, unattached to the power lead. He had evidently, simply forgotten to make that one, final, and vital connection.

Forgotten . . . ? His finger began to tremble. He dropped down limply on the seat-surface facing Annie.

He had not forgotten. Not just . . . forgotten. A man did not forget something like that. It was a lifetime's moral training against murder that had tripped him up. And his squeamishness would, in the long run, probably cost the lives of everyone alive on Earth at this moment.

He was sitting—staring at his hands, when the sound of the door opening brought him to his feet. He whirled about to see Mial.

It was not yet too late. The thought raced through his brain as all his muscles tensed. He could still try to kill the other man with his bare hands—and that was a job where his civilized upbringing could not trip him up. He shifted his weight on to his forward foot preparatory to hurling himself at Mial's throat. But before he could act, Mial spoke.

"Well," said the dark-haired man, harshly, "we did it."

Ty froze——checked by the single small word, *we*.

"We?" He stared at Mial, "Did what?"

"What do you think? The Chedal and the Laburti are going to agree—they'll sign a pact for the equivalent of a hundred and twenty-five years of peaceful cooperation, provided matters develop according to the instrument's estimates. They've got to check with their respective governments, of course, but that's only a formality—'' he broke off, his face tightening suspiciously. "What's wrong with you?" His gaze went past Ty to the open side of Annie.

"What's wrong with the instrument?"

"Nothing," said Ty. His head was whirling and he felt an insane urge to break out laughing. "—Annie just didn't kill you, that's all."

"Kill me?" Mial's face paled, then darkened. "You were going to kill me—with that?" He pointed at Annie.

"I was going to send thirteen thousand volts through you while you were helping me with the Demonstration," said Ty, still light-headed, "—if I hadn't crossed myself up. But you tell me it's all right, anyway. You say the aliens're going to agree."

"You thought they wouldn't?" said Mial, staring at him.

"I thought you were playing some game of your own. You said you were."

"That's right," said Mial. Some of the dark color faded from his face. "I was. I had to. You couldn't be trusted."

"*I* couldn't be trusted?" Ty burst out.

"Not you—or any of your bunch!" Mial laughed, harshly. "Babes in the woods, all of you. You build a machine that proves peace pays better than war, and think that settles the problem. What would have happened without someone like me along—"

"You! How they let someone like you weasel your way in—"

"Why you don't think I was assigned to this mission through any kind of accident, do you?" Mial laughed in Ty's face. "They combed the world to find someone like me."

"Combed the world? Why?"

"Because you *had* to come, and the Laburti would

113

only allow two of us with the analyzer to make the trip," said Mial. "You were the best Operator. But you were no politician—and no actor. And there was no time to teach you the facts of life. The only way to make it plain to the aliens that you were at cross purposes with me was to pick someone to head this Mission whom you couldn't help fighting."

"Couldn't help fighting?" Ty stood torn with fury and disbelief. "Why should I have someone along I couldn't help fighting—"

"So the aliens would believe me when I told them your faction back on Earth was strong enough so that I had to carry on the real negotiations behind your back."

"What—real negotiations?"

"Negotiations," said Mial, "to decide whose side we with our Annie-machines and their Operators would be on during the hundred and twenty-five years of peace between the Great Races." Mial smiled sardonically at Ty.

"Side?" Ty stood staring at the other man. "Why should we be on anyone's side?"

"Why, because by manipulating the data fed to the analyzers, we can control the pattern of growth; so that the Chedal can gain three times as fast as the Laburti in a given period, or the Laburti gain at the same rate over the Chedal. Of course," said Mial, dryly, "I didn't ever exactly promise we could do that in so many words, but they got the idea. Of course, it was the Laburti we had to close with—but I dickered with the Chedal first to get the Laburti price up."

"What price?"

"Better relationships, more travel between the races."

"But—" Ty stammered. "It's not true! That about manipulating the data."

"Of course it's not true!" snapped Mial. "And they never would have believed it if they hadn't seen you—the neutralist—fighting me like a Kilkenny cat." Mial stared at him. "Neither alien bunch ever thought seriously about not going to war anyway. They each just considered putting it off until they could go into it with a greater advantage over the other."

"But—they can't *prefer* war to peace!"

Mial made a disgusted noise in his throat.

"You amateur statesman!" he said. "You build a better mousetrap and you think that's all there is to it. Just because something's better for individuals, or races, doesn't mean they'll automatically go for it. The Chedal and Laburti have a reason for going to war that can't be figured on your Annie-machine."

"What?" Ty was stung.

"It's called the emotional factor," said Mial, grimly. "The climate of feeling that exists between the Chedal and the Laburti races—like the climate between you and me."

Ty found his gaze locked with the other man's. He opened his mouth to speak—then closed it again. A cold, electric shock of knowledge seemed to flow through him. Of course, if the Laburti felt about the Chedal as he felt about Mial . . .

All at once, things fell together for him, and he saw the true picture with painfully clear eyes. But the sudden knowledge was a tough pill to get down. He hesitated.

"But you've just put off war a hundred and twenty-five years!" he said. "And both alien races'll be twice as strong, then!"

"And we'll be forty times as strong as we are now," said Mial, dryly. "What do you think a nearly three per cent growth advantage amounts to, compounded over a hundred and twenty-five years? By that time we'll be strong enough to hold the balance of power between them and force peace, if we want it. They'd like to cut each other's throats, all right, but not at the cost of cutting their own, for sure. Besides," he went on, more slowly, "if your peace can prove itself in that length of time—now's its chance to do it."

He fell silent. Ty stood, feeling betrayed and ridiculed. All the time he had been suspecting Mial, the other man had been working clear-eyed toward the goal. For if the Laburti and the Chedal felt as did he and Mial, the unemotional calm sense of Annie's forecast never would have convinced the aliens to make peace.

Ty saw Mial watching him now with a sardonic smile. He thinks I haven't got the guts to congratulate him, thought Ty.

"All right," he said, out loud. "You did a fine job—in spite of me. Good for you."

"Thanks," said Mial grimly. They looked at each other.

"But—" said Ty, after a minute, between his teeth, the instinctive venom in him against the other man rushing up behind his words, "I still hate your guts! Once I thought there was a way out of that, but you've convinced me different, as far as people like us are concerned. Once this is over, I hope to heaven I never set eyes on you again!"

Their glances met nakedly.

"Amen," said Mial softly. "Because next time *I'll* kill you."

"Unless I beat you to it," said Ty.

Mial looked at him a second longer, then turned and quit the room. From then on, and all the way back to Earth they avoided each other's company and did not speak again. For there was no need of any more talk.

They understood each other very well.

Rehabilitated

I went into a bar.

"Gimme a drink," I said to the bartender.

"Brother, don't take that drink," said a voice at my elbow. I turned and there was a skinny little guy in his fifties. Thin, yellow hair and a smile on his face. "Brother, don't take that drink," he said.

I shook him off.

"Where'd you come from?" I said. "You weren't there when I sat down here one second ago." He just grinned at me.

"Gimme a drink," I said to the bartender.

"Not for you," said the bartender. "You had enough before you came in here." A fat bartender polishing shot glasses with his little finger inside a dishtowel. "Get your friend to take you home."

"He's no friend of mine," I said.

"Brother," said the little man, "come with me."

"I want a drink," I said. An idea struck me. I turned to the little man. "Let's you and I go someplace else and have a drink," I said.

We went out of the bar together, and suddenly we were somewhere else.

After I started to get over it, it wasn't too bad. The first week was bad, but after that it got better. When I found how the little man had trapped me, I tried to get away from the mission or whatever it was he'd taken me to. But after the booze died out I was real weak and sick for a long time. And after that stage was over I got to feeling that maybe I would quit after all. And I started having long talks with the little man. His name was Peer Ambrose.

"How old are you, Jack?" he asked me.

"Twenty-six," I said.

He looked at me with tight little brown eyes in his leather face, grinning.

"Can you run an elevator, Jack?"

"I can run any damn thing!" I said, getting mad.

"Can you, Jack?" he said, not turning a hair.

"Whattayou mean, can I run an elevator?" I shouted at him. "Any flying fool can run an elevator. I can run any damn thing, and you ask me can I run an elevator. Sure I can run an elevator!"

"I have one I'd like you to run for me," he said.

"Well, all right," I said. I didn't mean to yell at him. He didn't seem to be a bad little man; but he was always grinning at me.

So I went to work running the elevator. It wasn't bad. It gave me something to do around the mission or whatever it was. But it wasn't enough to do, and I got bored. I never could understand why they didn't have one of the automatics, anyway—any elevator with an operator was a museum piece.

But we were only about half a mile from the spaceport, and when there wasn't anything doing I'd take the elevator up to the transparent weather bubble that opened on the roof garden and watch the commuters and the sky with its clouds and the big ships taking off all sharp and black like a black penpoint at the end of a long white cone of exhaust. I didn't do much—just sat and watched them. When the signal rang in the elevator, I'd press the studs and we'd float down the tube to whatever floor wanted an elevator, and that'd be that.

After a few weeks, old Peer rang for me one day on

the office level and told me to leave the elevator and come on in to his office. When I went in with him there was another man there, a young man with black hair and wearing a business cut on his jacket.

"Jack," said Peer, "this is counselor Toby Gregg. Toby, this is Jack Heimelmann. Jack's been with us for over a month now."

"Is that a fact?" said Toby. "Well, I'm glad to meet you, Jack." He put out his hand, but I didn't take it.

"What's this?" I asked, looking at Peer. "What're you cooking up for me now?"

"Jack," said Peer, putting his hand on my arm and looking up into my face, "you need help. You know that. And Gregg here has training that'll help him give it to you."

"I don't know about that," I said.

"Jack," said Peer, "you know I wouldn't recommend anything that was bad for you. Now, I'm going to ask you to talk to Gregg. Just talk to him."

Well, I gave in. Peer said he'd get somebody else for the elevator and I was to come and talk to Gregg three times a week, and meantime I was to be given some books to read.

The first time I went to see Gregg in his office on office level, he offered me a drink.

"A drink!" I said. And right away the old thirst came charging up. And then, while I stood there, it faded again, all by itself.

"I guess not," I said. Then I stared at him. "What's the idea of offering me a drink?" I asked. "What're you trying to do?"

"I'm just proving something to you, Jack," he said. We were sitting in a couple of slope-back easy chairs with a little low table between us that fitted up against one wall of the office. He reached over and pressed a stud on the table and a little panel in the wall above the table opened and a bottle and some glasses slid out on a tray. "Go ahead, you can have the drink if you want. I'm just showing you that it isn't your drinking that we have to fix, but what's behind it. When we get through with you, you'll be able to take a drink without going out on a bender."

"I will?" I said. I looked at the tray. "I still guess I won't have anything."

"Cigarette?" he said, offering me one.

I took that.

"Tell me, Jack," he said, when I had the cigarette going between my lips, "how long have you been smoking, now?"

"Why," I told him, "let's see. I was smoking in general prep school when I was twelve. That'd be . . . let's see . . ."

"Fourteen years," he said. "That's a long time. You started early. You must have had a pretty rough bunch of kids around that general prep."

"Bunch of damn sissies," I told him. "Catch *them* smoking! I bet there isn't a dozen of them that smoke today."

"Most people don't, you know," said Gregg.

"My dad started at ten," I said.

"That was back a few years," he smiled. "Habits change with the years, Jack. Most of those kids you were in school with were probably looking forward to jobs where smoking wouldn't be practical."

"Yeah. Yeah, I bet they were," I said. "They sure figured to be big shots."

"All of them?" he asked.

"Most of them," I said. This talk was getting on my nerves. I didn't like to talk about general prep school. I had five years of it after I got out of secondary and I was seventeen before I cut loose. And that was plenty.

"Didn't you have a few friends?" he asked.

"Hell, yes!" I said. "D'you think I was an introvert?"

"No, Jack," he said, soothingly. "I can tell by looking at you you're not an introvert. But these friends of yours. Do you ever see any of them any more?"

I jumped up out of the chair.

"Listen, what is this?" I shouted at him. "What're you getting at? What're you trying to find out? I don't see any sense to this kind of questioning. I don't have to sit and listen to these kind of stupid questions. I'm leaving."

And I turned and headed toward the office door.

"All right, Jack," he said behind me, not irritated at all. "Come back any time you feel like it."

At the door, I turned once more to look at him. But he had his back to me. He was putting the tray with the bottles and glasses on it back into the wall.

I told Peer I had changed my mind about the counseling and went back to work on the elevator. The old man didn't seem annoyed at all. And I worked on the elevator for several weeks, riding people up and down and going up by myself to watch the sky and the people flying around and the ships. But after a while it began to wear on me.

I don't know what actually made me decide to go back to Gregg. I suppose it was because there just wasn't anything else. There was nothing much doing with the elevator, and there wasn't much sense in leaving the place and going back to the old drinking again. I really didn't want to start that all over again, but I knew if I got out by myself I would. Finally I figured I'd go back to Gregg and tell him I'd listen to just enough questions to cure me of my drinking, but nothing else.

When I went back to see him for the first time, though, he told me that wouldn't work.

"You see, Jack," he told me, "to get rid of the drinking, we have to get rid of whatever it is that's making you want to drink. And whatever that is, it's what's causing all your other troubles. So, it's up to you whether you want a complete job done or not."

I thought for a minute. Somehow talking with him made it seem easy.

"Oh, hell!" I said, finally. "Let's dig it out. I can't be any worse off, anyway."

*   *   *

So we went to it. And it was one rough time. Even Gregg said it was rougher than he figured. At first I was always blowing up and stamping out. But I finally got to the point where I could tell him anything. And it came out that I'd started getting a chip on my shoulder back as a kid because I thought the other kids were better than I was. Actually, Gregg said, it was my adverse environment that was hampering me. My mother was a state ward because of her unstable mental condition, and the only woman we had around the house was the housekeeper Government Service paid for. My dad was a portable-operating-room driver for a country hospital, and he was away from home on calls most of the time. He wanted me to be a driver like him when I got out of school, but by that time they had the automatic routers in, so I didn't.

But Gregg figured out that, even though I never really liked the idea, my dad wanting me to do a manual job had given me an inferiority complex. Like my driving a portable operating room, when all the other kids in school were looking forward to being Earthside deskmen, or professionals, or getting schooled for new-world trades; the sort of work that means learning half a dozen different lines that'll be needed on a new planet. Gregg figured it started hitting me as soon as I got into prep school and that was why I got into all kinds of trouble with the instructors and ran with a knify bunch and took up smoking and drinking. And he said that my inferiority complex had made me believe that I hated work; while actually, I was just taking out my dislike for my classmates on it. He said it was quite to be expected under those conditions that I would just come out of prep school and draw my social maintenance year after year without really trying to find anything to do. And then, as time went on, the drink was bound to start to get me.

Anyway we went back over all my life and he started pointing out to me where I had been wrong in thinking I wasn't as good as the other kids; and after a while I began to see it myself. And from that time on I began actually to change.

It's not easy to explain just what it was like. I had had a basically good schooling, as Gregg pointed out, and with the learning techniques used in our modern schools, the knowledge was all there, still. I had just not been using it. Now, as we talked together, he began to remind me of little odds and ends of things. My vocabulary increased and my reading speed picked up. He had me study intensively; and though at some times it was real hard, little by little I began to talk and act like someone of professional, or at least desk level.

"What you need now," Gregg said to me one day, "is to decide on some specific plan of action."

"I beg your pardon?" I said, puzzled.

"A job, or some work you can devote yourself to," said Gregg. "You've been refusing to face the fact for years, but in our modern society everyone is busy at their chosen work. Now, what would you like to do?"

I stared at him.

"Have you ever thought of emigrating, for instance?" he went on. "You're large and young and strong and— active-natured. The new-world life might suit you."

I thought about it.

"The new worlds aren't like Earth," Gregg went on. "We're overstocked here on second-raters, bogged down in a surplus of inferior talent. All the bright young men and women in each generation graduate and get off planet as quickly as they can. On a newer world, you'd be free, Jack. Your social unit would be smaller, and your personal opportunity to develop greater. It'd mean a lot of hard work, of course."

"I wouldn't mind that," I said.

While he talked, I had been thinking. I remembered the teachers teaching about the new worlds in prep school. Hitherto untouched planets, they'd told us, which in every case present a great challenge and offer a great reward to the pioneer. Twenty-four percent of our young people emigrating every year. That meant, of course, the ones who had completed their schooling and passed the physical. The more I thought of it, the better it sounded for me.

"I'd like to leave Earth," I said. "There's nothing for me here."

"Well, good," said Gregg. "If your mind's made up, then you've come a long way from the man I first met. You know you'll have to go back to school and get your certificate?"

"Sure. I know."

"Fine," said Gregg. He punched some buttons. "We'll start you tomorrow. Well, I guess that's enough for today."

He got up and went with me to the door and out into the main corridor of office level. Coming down the hall was Peer, and he had a little girl with brown hair with him. They stopped to talk with us and I got introduced to the girl. That was the first time I met Leena Tore.

I liked Leena a lot.

I had bumped into a lot of women in the past years; but either they had been no-goods, hitting the alcohol as hard as I was, or else they were stuck up and you couldn't get along with them. I'd seen them once or twice, but we wouldn't get along and that would be the limit. They all talked too much and looked down on anybody who wasn't professional level at least.

Leena wasn't like that. She didn't talk too much; and to tell the truth, she wasn't bright at all. In fact, she was stupid. But we got along very well together. She was an orphan, raised under State supervision in a private home. They found a job for her when she got old enough, but she didn't like it and finally went on social maintenance, and didn't do anything but sit around and watch shows all day. Finally Peer heard of her and brought her down to the place.

Gregg was working with her, too. But he hadn't been going on her long enough to make any real difference, and, privately, I didn't think he ever would. She was really too stupid. But she was an easy sort of person to get along with and after a while I began to think of marrying her.

Meanwhile, I was going back to school. It was hard

as hell—I'd forgotten how hard it was. But then I hadn't really worked at it before, and I'd been away from the preliminary stuff a long time.

But I'd been through it all once before, as Gregg reminded me—I'd forgotten—which helped; and they really do have good techniques and associative equipment in the schools nowadays. So after a while, I began to know my stuff and it perked me up. And when I got stuck Gregg would talk to me, and then things would come easy.

I got myself some new clothes and I began to mix with my classmates. Most of them were young kids, but by keeping my mouth shut I got along with them pretty well. And, you know, I began to feel this stuff they talk about, the sense of personal and racial destiny. I'd look around at these tall, good-looking kids talking big about the stars and the future. And then I'd look at myself in the mirror and say, "Boy, you're part of all this." And I began to see what Gregg had said my inferiority complex had cut me off from before.

They said Leena was making progress. She had been going to school too, but she was several classes behind me and she still had some time to go when I graduated. So we talked it over, all four of us, Leena and me, and Peer and Gregg, and we decided I'd go ahead and get cleared and ship out for some world. And then when Leena came along later she could just specify the same destination when she went through emigration.

Leena didn't look too pleased at having to wait. She pouted a bit, then finally gave in. But I was eager to go. These past months had gotten me thoroughly into the mood of emigration, and I was a happy man the day I went down to the big section outside the spaceport where clearing and routing went on for those who went spaceward from our city. Gregg had had a long talk with me, and I felt real good.

There wasn't to be too much to it. I presented my certificate of graduation and my credentials. The deskman glanced them over and asked me if I had any preference about examiners.

"Celt Winter," I said. This was the man Peer and Gregg had told me to ask for. They said he was a friend of Gregg's who had heard about me from Gregg and was very interested in me. It seems he didn't have much time off, ordinarily, so he never had any chance to drop around the place; and if I asked for him as my examiner, that would give us a chance to meet before I left.

The deskman ran his finger down his file and pressed a few studs. A message jumped out on the screen set in his desk.

"Celt Winter has just stepped out for a minute," he said. "Do you want to wait, or shall I give you someone else?"

I sort of hesitated. I hated to disappoint this Winter, but I was too wound up just to sit and twiddle my thumbs until he got back. I saw the deskman looking at me, waiting for my answer, and I got kind of nervous.

"Oh, anyone'll do," I said. "Just give me anybody that's free."

"Sven Coleman, then," said the deskman. "Desk four sixty-two." He gave me a little plastic tab and directed me through a door to his right.

I went through the door and came out into a big hall covered with desks at which examiners sat. Most of them had people sitting with them. I went ahead down a lane between the desks until I reached the four-sixty row, and two places off to my right I came to a desk where a tall young deskman with black hair and a long, straight nose waved me to a seat.

I handed him my credentials: my graduation certificate, my government registration card, and my physical okay sheet, for I'd taken that exam a couple of days before. He read through them.

"Well, Mr. Heimelmann," he said, smiling at me, and laying the credentials down. "You realize this is just a sort of formality. We interviewers are set up here just for the purpose of making sure that those of our people who go out to the new worlds won't want to turn back when they get there. In fact, this is just a last-minute chance for you to change your mind."

"There's no danger of that," I said.

He smiled and nodded.

"That's fine," he said. "Now perhaps you'd like to tell me, Mr. Heimelmann, what you particularly want to do when you get to your pioneer world and any preferences you might have as to location."

Gregg had told me that they'd ask me that, and I had my answer ready.

"I'd like to get out on the edge of things," I said. "I like singleton jobs. As for location, any place that's got plenty of outdoors is fine."

He laughed.

"Well, we can certainly suit those preferences," he said. "Most of our prospective emigrants are looking forward to team work in a close colony."

I laughed, too. I found myself liking this man.

"Probably afraid to get their feet wet," I said.

His smile went a little puzzled. Then he laughed again.

"I see what you mean," he said. "Too much community emphasis is a bad thing, even though the motives are good."

"Sure," I said. "If you like a crowd, you might as well stay here on Earth."

He looked puzzled again, and then serious. He picked up my credentials and went through them once more.

"You're in your late twenties, aren't you, Mr. Heimelmann?" he said.

"That's right," I answered.

"But I see that according to your graduation certificate, you just finished your trade learnings."

"Oh," I said. "Well, you see, I fooled around for a few years there. I couldn't seem to make up my mind about what I wanted to do."

"I see," he said. He put down my credentials and sat for a moment, tapping the top of the desk with his forefinger and looking as if he was thinking. "Excuse me a moment, Mr. Heimelmann."

He got up and left. After a few minutes he was back. "Will you come with me, please?" he asked.

I wondered a bit, but I got up and followed him. I didn't see any of the other interviewers doing this with the people they had at their desks. But you can't tell what the procedure is in these kind of places by just looking. Sven Coleman took me over to one side of the big room and through a door into an office where a sort of nervous older-looking man got up from a desk to greet us.

"Mr. Heimelmann," said Coleman. "This is Mr. Jos Alter. He'd like to talk to you for a moment."

"Hello," I said, shaking hands.

"How do you do, Mr. Heimelmann," answered Alter. "Sit down beside my desk here, will you? That'll be all, Sven."

"Yes, sir," said Coleman and went out. I followed Alter to the desk and sat down. He had two tired lines between his eyes and a little mustache.

"Mr. Heimelmann," he said. "I've got a little test here I want you to take. I'm going to give you a tape and I'd like you to take it over to the machine there and put it in. As the questions pop up on the screen, you press either the true stud or the false to register your choice. Will you do that? I've got to step out for a minute, but I'll be right back."

And he handed me the tape. It all seemed sort of strange to me, but as Sven himself said, this business was just a formality. I did what Alter wanted me to.

The questions were easy at first. If I have ten credits and I give two-thirds of them away, how many do I have left? If the main traffic strips are closed to children below the age of responsibility and I have a five-year-old nephew with me, can I send him home alone? But after a while they began to get harder, and I was still working when Alter came back. He took the tape and we went back to his desk, where he ran it through a scorer and set it aside. Then he just looked at me.

"Mr. Heimelmann," he said, finally. "Where've you spent the last six months or a year?"

"Why, at the place," I said. "I mean, the Freemen Independent Foundation Center."

"I see," he said. "And will you tell me briefly how you happened to go there in the first place and what you've been doing while you were there?"

I hesitated. There was something strange about all this. But I had to give him some answer, and there was no point in telling him anything but the truth when he could just press a stud on his desk and call Peer to ask him.

"Well," I said, squirming some inside, for it isn't easy to admit you've been an alcoholic, "I was drinking one day in a bar. . . ."

And I went through the whole story for him, down to the present. After I'd finished, he sat for a long while without saying anything. I didn't say anything, either. I was feeling pretty low down after admitting what I'd been. Finally he spoke.

"Blast those people!" he said, viciously. "Blast and damn them!"

I stared at him.

"Who?" I said. "Who? I don't understand."

He turned and looked me full in the face.

"Mr. Heimelmann," he said, "your friends at the Foundation—" he hesitated. "Nobody hates to tell you this more than I do, but the fact of the matter is we can't approve you for emigration."

"Can't?" I echoed. His words seemed to roar in my ears. The room tilted and I seemed to have a sudden feeling as if I was falling, falling from a great, high place. And all the time I knew I was just sitting beside his desk. I grabbed at the desk to steady myself. I had a terrible feeling then as if everybody was marching away and leaving me—all the tall young people I'd gone to classes and graduated with. But I *had* graduated. My credentials were in order.

"Listen," I said; and I had to struggle to get the words out. "I'm qualified."

129

"I'm sorry," he said. And he did look sorry—sorry enough to cry. "You're not, Mr. Heimelmann. You're totally unfit, and your friends at the Foundation knew it. This isn't the first time they've tried to slip somebody by us, counting on the fact that modern education can get facts into anybody."

I just looked at him. I tried to say something, but my throat was too tight and the words wouldn't come out.

"Mr. Heimelmann . . . Jack . . ." he said. "I'll try and explain it to you, though it's not my job and I really don't know how. You see, in many ways, Jack, you're much better off than your ancestors. You're in perfect physical health. You're taller and stronger. You have faster reflexes and better coordination. You're much better balanced mentally, so much so, in fact, that it would be almost impossible for you to go insane, or even to develop a severe psychosis, but—"

I tasted blood in my mouth, but there was no pain. The room was beginning to haze up around me, and I felt something like a time bomb beginning to swell and tick in the back of my brain. His voice roared at me like out of a hurricane.

"—you have an IQ of ninety-two, Jack. Once upon a time this wasn't too bad, but in our increasingly technical civilization—" he spread his hands helplessly.

The hurricane was getting worse. I could hardly hear him now and I could hardly see the room. I felt the time bomb trembling, ready to explode.

"What these people at the Foundation did to you," he was saying, "was to use certain psi techniques to excite your own latent psi talents—a procedure which isn't yet illegal, but shortly will be. This way, they were able to sensitize you to amounts and types of knowledge you wouldn't otherwise be able to absorb—in much the same way we train animals, using these psi techniques, to perform highly complicated actions. Like an animal——"

The world split wide open. When I could see again, I found little old, leather-face Peer had joined us in the room. Alter was slumped in his chair, his eyes closed.

Peer crossed over to him, looked him over, then glanced at me with a low whistle.

"Easy, Jack," he said. "Easy now. . . ." And I suddenly realized I was trembling like a leaf. But with his words, the tension began to go. Peer was shaking his head at me.

"We got a shield on Alter just in time," he said. "He's just going to wake up thinking you left and he dozed off for a while. But you don't realize what kind of a mental punch you've got, Jack. You would have killed him if I hadn't protected him."

For the first time, that came home to me. My hurricane could have killed Alter. I understood that, now. My knees weakened.

"No, it's all right. He's just out temporarily," said Peer. "Unfreeze yourself, Jack, and we'll teleport out of here. . . . What's the matter?"

"I want to know——" the words came hard from my throat. "I want to know, right now. What'd you do to me?"

Peer sighed.

"Can't it wait?—no, I guess not," he said, looking at me. "If you must know, you were an experiment. The first of your particular kind. But there'll be lots like you from now on; we'll see to that. Earth is starving, Jack; starving for the very minds and talents and skills it ships out each year. It's behind the times now and falling further every year, because the first-class young people all emigrate and the culls are left behind."

"Thanks!" I said, between my teeth and with my fists clenched. "Thanks a lot."

"Why not face facts?" said Peer cheerfully. "You're a high-grade moron, Jack—no, don't try that on me, what you did on Alter," he added, as I took a step forward. "You're not that tough, yet, Jack, though someday we hope you may be. As I was saying, you're a high-grade moron. Me, I've got an aneurysm that can't stand any kind of excitement, let alone spaceflight. Gregg, for your information, has a strong manic-depressive pattern—and so on, at the Foundation.''

"I don't know what you mean," I said, sullenly.

"Of course you don't. But you will, Jack, you will," said Peer. "A government of second-raters were afraid to trigger your kind of talent in a high-grade moron, so they passed restrictive laws. We've just proved that triggering your abilities can not only be safe but practical. More evidence for a change that's coming here on Earth."

"You lied to me!" I shouted, suddenly. "All the time you were lying to me! All of you!"

"Well, now, we had to," Peer said. "It required a blockbuster of an emotional shock to break through all the years of conditioning that told you someone like yourself couldn't compete. You had to be so frustrated on a normal level that you'd go to your abnormal powers in desperation. Your desire to get off Earth to a place where life would be different was real enough. Gregg just built it up to where you couldn't face being turned down. And then we arranged the turn-down."

I was crying.

"You shouldn't have done it!" I said. "You shouldn't have! For the first time, I thought I had some friends. For the first time——"

"Who says we're not your friends?" snapped Peer. "You think we went to all that trouble to break the law and bust you loose without figuring that you could be as close to us as anyone in the world could be? You—well, there's no use trying to explain it to you. You've got to be shown. Lock on, gang!"

And suddenly—they did lock on. For a second, I almost fell over, I was so scared. I felt Peer's mind slip into mine, then Toby Greggs's—and, without warning, there too was Leena. And she was not the same Leena I knew at all, but somebody almost as bright as Gregg. Only she was an epileptic.

All of a sudden, I knew too much. I heaved, with all the strength that was in me, trying to break loose. But the three of them held me easily.

"You just want to use me!" I shouted at them—with my mouth and my mind, both. "You just want me for what I can do for you—like a big, stupid horse." I was crying again, this time internally as well. "Just because you're all smarter than I am and you can make me do what you say!"

"Calm down, Jack," came the thought of Toby. "You've got the picture all wrong. What kind of a team is that, the three of us riding on your back? What do you think keeps Peer nicely calmed down all the time? And what do you think keeps Leena's epileptic attacks under control and me sane? Let me show you something."

And then he did something which was for me like heaven opening up and showing a rainbow in all its glory to a blind man.

"You want a few extra IQ points to think with?" said Toby. "Take mine!"

Lulungomeena

Blame Clay Harbank, if you will, for what happened at Station 563 of the Sirius Sector; or blame William Peterborough, whom we called the Kid. I blame no one. But I am a Dorsai man.

The trouble began the day the kid joined the station, with his quick hands and his gambler's mind, and found that Clay, alone of all the men there, would not gamble with him—for all that he claimed to having been a gambling man himself. And so it ran on for four years of service together.

But the beginning of the end was the day they came off shift together.

They had been out on a duty circuit of the frontier station that housed the twenty of us—searching the outer bubble for signs of blows or leaks. It's a slow two hour tramp, that duty, even outside the station on the surface of the asteroid where there's no gravity to speak of. We, in the recreation room, off duty, could tell by the sound of their voices as the inner port sucked open and the clanging clash of them removing their spacesuits came echoing to us along the metal corridor, that the Kid had been needling Clay through the whole tour.

"Another day," came the Kid's voice, "another fifty credits. And how's the piggy bank coming along, Clay?"

There was a slight pause, and I could see Clay carefully controlling his features and his voice. Then his pleasant baritone, softened by the burr of his Tarsusian accent, came smoothly to us.

"Like a gentleman, Kid," he answered. "He never overeats and so he runs no danger of indigestion."

It was a neat answer, based on the fact that the Kid's own service account was swollen with his winnings from the rest of the crew. But the Kid was too thick-skinned for rapier thrusts. He laughed; and they finished removing their equipment and came on into the recreation room.

They made a striking picture as they entered, for they were enough alike to be brothers—although father and son would have been a more likely relationship, considering the difference in their ages. Both were tall, dark, wide-shouldered men with lean faces, but experience had weathered the softer lines from Clay's face and drawn thin parentheses about the corners of his mouth. There were other differences, too; but you could see in the Kid the youth that Clay had been, and in Clay the man that the Kid would some day be.

"Hi, Clay," I said.

"Hello, Mort," he said, sitting down beside me.

"Hi, Mort," said the Kid.

I ignored him; and for a moment he tensed. I could see the anger flame up in the ebony depths of his black pupils under the heavy eyebrows. He was a big man; but I come from the Dorsai Planets and a Dorsai man fights to the death, if he fights at all. And, in consequence, among ourselves, we of Dorsai are a polite people.

But politeness was wasted on the Kid—as was Clay's delicate irony. With men like the Kid, you have to use a club.

We were in bad shape. The twenty of us at Frontier Station 563, on the periphery of the human area just beyond Sirius, had gone sour, and half the men had applications in for transfer. The trouble between Clay and the Kid was splitting the station wide open.

We were all in the Frontier Service for money; that

was the root of the trouble. Fifty credits a day is good pay—but you have to sign up for a ten year hitch. You can buy yourself out—but that costs a hundred thousand. Figure it out for yourself. Nearly six years if you saved every penny you got. So most go in with the idea of staying the full decade.

That was Clay's idea. He had gambled most of his life away. He had won and lost several fortunes. Now he was getting old and tired and he wanted to go back—to Lulungomeena, on the little planet of Tarsus, which was the place he had come from as a young man.

But he was through with gambling. He said money made that way never stuck, but ran away again like quicksilver. So he drew his pay and banked it.

But the Kid was out for a killing. Four years of play with the rest of the crew had given him more than enough to buy his way out and leave him a nice stake. And perhaps he would have done just that, if it hadn't been that the Service account of Clay's drew him like an El Dorado. He could not go off and leave it. So he stayed with the outfit, riding the older man unmercifully.

He harped continually on two themes. He pretended to disbelieve that Clay had ever been a gambler; and he derided Lulungomeena, Clay's birthplace: the older man's goal and dream, and the one thing he could be drawn into talk about. For, to Clay, Lulungomeena was beautiful, the most wonderful spot in the Universe; and with an old man's sick longing for home, he could not help saying so.

"Mort," said the Kid, ignoring the rebuff and sitting down beside us, "what's a Hixabrod like?"

My club had not worked so well, after all. Perhaps, I, too, was slipping. Next to Clay, I was the oldest man on the crew, which was why we were close friends. I scowled at the Kid.

"Why?" I asked.

"We're having one for a visitor," he said.

Immediately, all talk around the recreation room ceased and all attention was focused on the Kid. All aliens had to

137

clear through a station like ours when they crossed the frontier from one of the other great galactic power groups into human territory. But isolated as Station 563 was, it was seldom an alien came our way, and when one did, it was an occasion.

Even Clay succumbed to the general interest. "I didn't know that," he said. "How'd you find out?"

"The notice came in over the receiver when you were down checking the atmosphere plant," answered the Kid with a careless wave of his hand. "I'd already filed it when you came up. What'll he be like, Mort?"

I had knocked around more than any of them—even Clay. This was my second stretch in the Service. I remembered back about twenty years, to the Denebian Trouble.

"Stiff as a poker," I said. "Proud as Lucifer, honest as sunlight and tight as a camel on his way through the eye of a needle. Sort of a humanoid, but with a face like a collie dog. You know the Hixabrodian reputation, don't you?"

Somebody at the back of the crowd said no, although they may have been doing it just to humor me. Like Clay with his Lulungomeena, old age was making me garrulous.

"They're the first and only mercenary ambassadors in the known Universe," I said. "A Hixabrod can be hired, but he can't be influenced, bribed or forced to come up with anything but the cold truth—and, brother, it's cold the way a Hixabrod serves it up to you. That's why they're so much in demand. If any kind of political dispute comes up, from planetary to inter-alien power group levels, both sides have to hire a Hixabrod to represent them in the discussions. That way they know the other side is being honest with them. The opposing Hixabrod is a living guarantee of that."

"He sounds good," said the Kid. "What say we get together and throw him a good dinner during his twenty-four hour stop-over?"

"You won't get much in the way of thanks from him," I grunted. "They aren't built that way."

"Let's do it anyway," said the Kid. "Be a little excitement for a change."

A murmur of approval ran through the room. I was outvoted. Even Clay liked the idea.

"Hixabrods eat what we eat, don't they?" asked the Kid, making plans. "Okay, then soups, salad, meats, champagne and brandy—" he ran on, ticking the items off on his fingers. For a moment, his enthusiasm had us all with him. But then, just at the end, he couldn't resist getting in one more dig at Clay.

"Oh, yes," he finished, "and for entertainment, you can tell him about Lulungomeena, Clay."

Clay winced—not obviously, but we all saw a shadow cross his face. Lulungomeena on Tarsus, his birthplace, held the same sort of obsession for him that his Service account held for the Kid; but he could not help being aware that he was prone to let his tongue run away on the subject of its beauty. For it was where he belonged, in the stomach-twisting, throat-aching way that sometimes only talk can relieve.

I was a Dorsai man and older than the rest. I understood. No one should make fun of the bond tying a man to his home world. It is as real as it is intangible. And to joke about it is cruel.

But the Kid was too young to know that yet. He was fresh from Earth—Earth, where none of the rest of us had been, yet which, hundreds of years before, had been the origin of us all. He was eager and strong and contemptuous of emotion. He saw, as the rest of us recognized also, that Clay's tendency to let his talk wander ever to the wonder of Lulungomeena was the first slight crack in what had once been a man of unflawed steel. It was the first creeping decay of age.

But, unlike the rest of us, who hid our boredom out of sympathy, the Kid saw here a chance to break Clay and his resolution to do no more gambling. So he struck out constantly at this one spot so deeply vital that Clay's self-possession was no defense.

Now, at this last blow, the little fires of anger gathered in the older man's eyes.

"That's enough," he said harshly. "Leave Lulungomeena out of the discussion."

"I'm willing to," said the Kid. "But somehow you keep reminding me of it. That and the story that you once were a gambler. If you won't prove the last one, how can you expect me to believe all you say about the first?"

The veins stood out on Clay's forehead; but he controlled himself.

"I've told you a thousand times," he said between his teeth. "Money made by gambling doesn't stick. You'll find that out for yourself one of these days."

"Words," said the Kid airily. "Only words."

For a second, Clay stood staring whitely at him, not even breathing. I don't know if the Kid realized his danger or cared, but I didn't breathe, either, until Clay's chest expanded and he turned abruptly and walked out of the recreation room. We heard his bootsteps die away down the corridor toward his room in the dormitory section.

Later, I braced the Kid about it. It was his second shift time, when most of the men in the recreation room had to go on duty. I ran the Kid to the ground in the galley where he was fixing himself a sandwich. He looked up, a little startled, more than a little on the defensive, as I came in.

"Oh, hi, Mort," he said with a pretty good imitation of casualness. "What's up?"

"You," I told him. "Are you looking for a fight with Clay?"

"No," he drawled with his mouth full. "I wouldn't exactly say that."

"Well, that's what you're liable to get."

"Look, Mort," he said, and then paused until he had swallowed. "Don't you think Clay's old enough to look after himself?"

I felt a slight and not unpleasant shiver run down between my shoulder-blades and my eyes began to grow hot. It was my Dorsai blood again. It must have showed on my face, for the Kid, who had been sitting negligently on one edge of the galley table, got up in a hurry.

"Hold on, Mort," he said. "Nothing personal."

I fought the old feeling down and said as calmly as I could, "I just dropped by to tell you something. Clay has been around a lot longer than you have. I'd advise you to lay off him."

"Afraid he'll get hurt?"

"No," I answered. "I'm afraid you will."

The Kid snorted with sudden laughter, half choking on his sandwich. "Now I get it. You think I'm too young to take care of myself."

"Something like that, but not the way you think. I want to tell you something about yourself and you don't have to say whether I'm right or wrong—you'll let me know without the words."

"Hold it," he said, turning red. "I didn't come out here to get psyched."

"You'll get it just the same. And it's not for you only—it's for all of us, because men thrown together as closely as we are choose up sides whenever there's conflict, and that's as dangerous for the rest of us as it is for you."

"Then the rest of you can stay out of it."

"We can't," I said. "What affects one of us affects us all. Now I'll tell you what you're doing. You came out here expecting to find glamor and excitement. You found monotony and boredom instead, not realizing that that's what space is like almost all the time."

He picked up his coffee container. "And now you'll say I'm trying to create my own excitement at Clay's expense. Isn't that the standard line?"

"I wouldn't know; I'm not going to use it, because that's not how I see what you're doing. Clay is adult enough to stand the monotony and boredom if they'll get him what he wants. He's also learned how to live with

141

others and with himself. He doesn't have to prove himself by beating down somebody either half or twice his age.''

He took a drink and set the container down on the table. ''And I do ''

''All youngsters do. It's their way of experimenting with their potentialities and relationships with other people. When they find that out, they can give it up—they're mature then—although some never do. I think you will, eventually. The sooner you stop doing it here, though, the better it'll be for you and us.''

''And if I don't?'' he challenged.

''This isn't college back on Earth or some other nice, safe home planet, where hazing can be a nuisance, but where it's possible to escape it by going somewhere else. There isn't any 'somewhere else' here. Unless the one doing the hazing sees how reckless and dangerous it is, the one getting hazed takes it as long as he can—and then something happens.''

''So it's Clay you're really worried about, after all.''

''Look, get it through your skull. Clay's a man and he's been through worse than this before. You haven't. If anybody's going to get hurt, it'll be you.''

He laughed and headed for the corridor door. He was still laughing as it slammed behind him. I let him go. There's no use pushing a bluff after it's failed to work.

The next day, the Hixabrod came. His name was Dor Lassos. He was typical of his race, taller than the tallest of us by half a head, with a light green skin and that impassive Hixabrodian canine face.

I missed his actual arrival, being up in the observation tower checking meteor paths. The station itself was well protected, but some of the ships coming in from time to time could have gotten in trouble with a few of the larger ones that slipped by us at intervals in that particular sector. When I did get free, Dor Lassos had already been assigned to his quarters and the time of official welcoming was over.

I went down to see him anyhow on the off-chance

that we had mutual acquaintances either among his race or mine. Both of our people are few enough in number, God knows, so the possibility wasn't too far-fetched. And, like Clay, I yearned for anything connected with my home.

"*Wer velt d'hatchen, Hixabrod—*" I began, walking into his apartment—and stopped short.

The Kid was there. He looked at me with an odd expression on his face.

"Do you speak Hixabrodian?" he asked incredulously.

I nodded. I had learned it on extended duty during the Denebian Trouble. Then I remembered my manners and turned back to the Hixabrod; but he was already started on his answer.

"*En gles Ter, I tu, Dorsaiven,*" returned the collie face, expressionlessly. "*Da Tr'amgen lang. Met zurres nebent?*"

"*Em getluc. Me mi Dorsai fene. Nono ne—ves luc Les Lassos?*"

He shook his head.

Well, it had been a shot in the dark anyway. There was only the faintest chance that he had known our old interpreter at the time of the Denebian Trouble. The Hixabrods have no family system of nomenclature. They take their names from the names of older Hixabrods they admire or like. I bowed politely to him and left.

It was not until later that it occurred to me to wonder what in the Universe the Kid could find to talk about with a Hixabrod.

I actually was worried about Clay. Since my bluff with the Kid had failed, I thought I might perhaps try with Clay himself. At first I waited for an opportune moment to turn up; but following the last argument with the Kid, he'd been sticking to his quarters. I finally scrapped the casual approach and went to see him.

I found him in his quarters, reading. It was a little shocking to find that tall, still athletic figure in a dressing gown like an old man, eyes shaded by the lean fingers of one long hand, poring over the little glow of a scanner with the lines unreeling before his eyes. But he looked up as I came in, and the smile on his face was the smile I had grown familiar with over four years of close living together.

"What's that?" I asked, nodding at the book scanner.

He set it down and the little light went out, the lines stopped unreeling.

"A bad novel," he said, smiling, "by a poor author. But they're both Tarsusian."

I took the chair he had indicated. "Mind if I speak straight out, Clay?"

"Go ahead," he invited.

"The Kid," I said bluntly. "And you. The two of you can't go on this way."

"Well, old fire-eater," answered Clay lightly, "what've you got to suggest?"

"Two things. And I want you to think both of them over carefully before answering. First, we see if we can't get up a nine-tenths majority here in the station and petition him out as incompatible."

Clay slowly shook his head. "We can't do that, Mort."

"I think I can get the signatures if I ask it," I said. "Everybody's pretty tired of him . . . They'd come across."

"It's not that and you know it," said Clay. "Transfer by petition isn't supposed to be prejudicial, but you and I know it is. He'd be switched to some hard-case station, get in worse trouble there, and end up in a penal post generally shot to hell. He'd know who to blame for it, and he'd hate us for the rest of his life."

"What of it? Let him hate us."

"I'm a Tarsusian. It'd bother me and I couldn't do it."

"All right," I said. "Dropping that, then, you've got nearly seven years in, total, and half the funds you need to buy out. I've got nearly enough saved, in spite of myself, to make up the rest. In addition, for your retirement, I'll sign over to you my pay for the three years I've got left.

Take that and get out of the Service. It isn't what you figured on having, but half a loaf . . ."

"And how about your homegoing?" he asked.

"Look at me."

He looked; and I knew what he was seeing—the broken nose, the scars, the lined face—the Dorsai face.

"I'll never go home," I said.

He sat looking at me for a long moment more, and I fancied I saw a little light burn deep in back of his eyes. But then the light went out and I knew that I'd lost with him, too.

"Maybe not," he said quietly. "But I'm not going to be the one that keeps you from it."

I left him to his book.

Shifts are supposed to run continuously, with someone on duty all the time. However, for special occasions, like this dinner we had arranged for the Hixabrod, it was possible, by getting work done ahead of time and picking the one four hour-stretch during the twenty-four when there were no messages or ships due in, to assemble everybody in the station on an off-duty basis.

So we were all there that evening, in the recreation room, which had been cleared and set up with a long table for the dinner. We finished our cocktails, sat down at the table and the meal began.

As it will, the talk during the various courses turned to things outside the narrow limits of our present lives. Remembrances of places visited, memories of an earlier life, and the comparison of experiences, some of them pretty weird, were the materials of which our table talk was built.

Unconsciously, all of us were trying to draw the Hixabrod out. But he sat in his place at the head of the table between Clay and myself, with the Kid a little farther down, preserving a frosty silence until the dessert had been disposed of and the subject of Media unexpectedly came up.

"—Media," said the Kid. "I've heard of Media. It's

a little planet, but it's supposed to have everything from soup to nuts on it in the way of life. There's one little life-form there that's claimed to contain something of value to every metabolism. It's called—let me see now—it's called—''

"It is called *nygti*," supplied Dor Lassos, suddenly, in a metallic voice. "A small quadruped with a highly complex nervous system and a good deal of fatty tissue. I visited the planet over eighty years ago, before it was actually opened up to general travel. The food stores spoiled and we had the opportunity of testing out the theory that it will provide sustenance for almost any kind of known intelligent being."

He stopped.

"Well?" demanded the Kid. "Since you're here to tell the story, I assume the animal kept you alive."

"I and the humans aboard the ship found the *nygti* quite nourishing," said Dor Lassos. "Unfortunately, we had several Micrushni from Polaris also aboard."

"And those?" asked someone.

"A highly developed but inelastic life-form," said Dor Lassos, sipping from his brandy glass. "They went into convulsions and died."

I had had some experience with Hixabrodian ways and I knew that it was not sadism, but a complete detachment that had prompted this little anecdote. But I could see a wave of distaste ripple down the room. No life-form is so universally well liked as the Micrushni, a delicate iridescent jellyfishlike race with a bent toward poetry and philosophy.

The men at the table drew away almost visibly from Dor Lassos. But that affected him no more than if they had applauded loudly. Only in very limited ways are the Hixabrod capable of empathy where other races are concerned.

"That's too bad," said Clay slowly. "I have always liked the Micrushni." He had been drinking somewhat heavily and the seemingly innocuous statement came out like a half-challenge.

Dor Lassos' cold brown eyes turned and rested on him. Whatever he saw, whatever conclusions he came to, however, were hidden behind his emotionless face.

"In general," he said flatly, "a truthful race."

That was the closest a Hixabrod could come to praise, and I expected the matter to drop there. But the Kid spoke up again.

"Not like us humans," he said. "Eh, Dor Lassos?"

I glared at him from behind Dor Lassos' head. But he went recklessly on.

"I said, 'Not like us humans, eh?' " he repeated loudly. The Kid had also apparently been drinking freely, and his voice grated on the sudden silence of the room.

"The human race varies," stated the Hixabrod emotionlessly. "You have some individuals who approach truth. Otherwise, the human race is not notably truthful."

It was a typical, deadly accurate Hixabrodian response. Dor Lassos would have answered in the same words if his throat was to have been cut for them the minute they left his mouth. Again, it should have shut the Kid up, and again it apparently failed.

"Ah, yes," said the Kid. "Some approach truth, but in general we are untruthful. But you see, Dor Lassos, a certain amount of human humor is associated with lies. Some of us tell lies just for fun."

Dor Lassos drank from his brandy glass and said nothing.

"Of course," the Kid went on, "sometimes a human thinks he's being funny with his lies when he isn't. Some lies are just boring, particularly when you're forced to hear them over and over again. But on the other hand, there are some champion liars who are so good that even you would find their untruths humorous."

Clay sat upright suddenly, and the sudden start of his movement sent the brandy slopping out over the rim of his glass and onto the white tablecloth. He stared at the Kid.

I looked at them all—at Clay, at the Kid and at Dor Lassos; and an ugly premonition began to form in my brain.

"I do not believe I should," said Dor Lassos.

"Ah, but you should listen to a real expert," said the Kid feverishly, "when he has a good subject to work on. Now, for example, take the matter of home worlds. What is your home world, Hixa, like?"

I had heard enough and more than enough to confirm the suspicion forming within me. Without drawing any undue attention to myself, I rose and left the room.

The alien made a dry sound in his throat and his voice followed me as I went swiftly down the empty corridor.

"It is very beautiful," he said in his adding machine tones. "Hixa has a diameter of thirty-eight thousand universal meters. It possesses twenty-three great mountain ranges and seventeen large bodies of salt water . . ."

The sound of his voice died away and I left it behind me.

I went directly through the empty corridors and up the ladder to the communications shack. I went in the door without pausing, without—in neglect of all duty rules—glancing at the automatic printer to see if any fresh message out of routine had arrived, without bothering to check the transmitter to see that it was keyed into the automatic location signal for approaching spacecraft.

All this I ignored and went directly to the file where the incoming messages are kept.

I flicked the tab and went back to the file of two days previous, skimming through the thick sheaf of transcripts under that dateline. And there, beneath the heading "Notices of Arrivals," I found it, the message announcing the coming of Dor Lassos. I ran my finger down past the statistics on our guest to the line of type that told me where the Hixabrod's last stop had been.

Tarsus.

Clay was my friend. And there is a limit to what a man can take without breaking. On a wall of the communications shack was a roster of the men at our station. I drew the Dorsai sign against the name of William Peterborough, and checked my gun out of the arms locker.

I examined the magazine. It was loaded. I replaced the magazine, put the gun inside my jacket, and went back to the dinner.

Dor Lassos was still talking.

". . . The flora and the fauna are maintained in such excellent natural balance that no local surplus has exceeded one per cent of the normal population for any species in the last sixty thousand years. Life on Hixa is regular and predictable. The weather is controlled within the greatest limits of feasibility."

As I took my seat, the machine voice of the Hixabrod hesitated for just a moment, then gathered itself, and went on: "One day I shall return there."

"A pretty picture," said the Kid. He was leaning forward over the table now, his eyes bright, his teeth bared in a smile. "A very attractive home world. But I regret to inform you, Dor Lassos, that I've been given to understand that it pales into insignificance when compared to one other spot in the Galaxy."

The Hixabrod are warriors, too. Dor Lassos' features remained expressionless, but his voice deepened and rang through the room.

"Your planet?"

"I wish it were," returned the Kid with the same wolfish smile. "I wish I could lay claim to it. But this place is so wonderful that I doubt if I would be allowed there. In fact," the Kid went on, "I have never seen it. But I have been hearing about it for some years now. And either it is the most wonderful place in the Universe, or else the man who has been telling me about it—"

I pushed my chair back and started to rise, but Clay's hand clamped on my arm and held me down.

"You were saying—" he said to the Kid, who had been interrupted by my movement.

"—The man who has been telling me about it," said the Kid, deliberately, "is one of those champion liars I was telling Dor Lassos about."

Once more I tried to get to my feet, but Clay was there before me. Tall and stiff, he stood at the end of the table.

"My right—" he said out of the corner of his mouth to me.

Slowly and with meaning, he picked up his brandy glass and threw the glass straight into the Kid's face. It bounced on the table in front of him and sent brandy flying over the front of the Kid's immaculate dress uniform.

"Get your gun!" ordered Clay.

Now the Kid was on his feet. In spite of the fact that I knew he had planned this, emotion had gotten the better of him at the end. His face was white with rage. He leaned on the edge of the table and fought with himself to carry it through as he had originally intended.

"Why guns?" he said. His voice was thick with restraint, as he struggled to control himself.

"You called me a liar."

"Will guns tell me if you are?" The Kid straightened up, breathing more easily; and his laugh was harsh in the room. "Why use guns when it's possible to prove the thing one way or another with complete certainty?" His gaze swept the room and came back to Clay.

"For years now you've been telling me all sorts of things," he said. "But two things you've told me more than all the rest. One was that you used to be a gambler. The other was that Lulungomeena—your precious Lulungomeena on Tarsus—was the most wonderful place in the Universe. Is either one of those the truth?"

Clay's breath came thick and slow.

"They're both the truth," he said, fighting to keep his voice steady.

"Will you back that up?"

"With my life!"

"Ah," said the Kid mockingly, holding up his forefinger, "but I'm not asking you to back those statements up with your life—but with that neat little hoard you've been accumulating these past years. You claimed you're a gambler. Will you bet that those statements are true?"

Now, for the first time, Clay seemed to see the trap.

"Bet with me," invited the Kid, almost lightly. "That will prove the first statement."

"And what about the second?" demanded Clay.

"Why—" the Kid gestured with his hand toward Dor Lassos—"what further judge do we need? We have here at our table a Hixabrod." Half-turning to the alien, the Kid made him a little bow. "Let him say whether your second statement is true or not."

Once more I tried to rise from my seat and again Clay's hand shoved me down. He turned to Dor Lassos.

"Do you think you could judge such a point, sir?" he asked.

The brown inhuman eyes met his and held for a long moment.

"I have just come from Tarsus," said the Hixabrod. "I was there as a member of the Galactic Survey Team, mapping the planet. It was my duty to certify to the truth of the map."

The choice was no choice. Clay stood staring at the Hixabrod as the room waited for his answer. Rage burning within me, I looked down the table for a sign in the faces of the others that this thing might be stopped. But where I expected to see sympathy, there was nothing. Instead, there was blankness, or cynicism, or even the wet-lipped interest of men who like their excitement written in blood or tears.

And I realized with a sudden sinking of hopes that I stood alone, after all, as Clay's friend. In my own approaching age and garrulity I had not minded his talk of Lulungomeena, hour on repetitive hour. But these others had grown weary of it. Where I saw tragedy, they saw only retribution coming to a lying bore.

And what Clay saw was what I saw. His eyes went dark and cold.

"How much will you bet?" he asked.

"All I've got," responded the Kid, leaning forward eagerly. "Enough and more than enough to match that bank roll of yours. The equivalent of eight years' pay."

Stiffly, without a word, Clay produced his savings book and a voucher pad. He wrote out a voucher for the whole amount and laid book and voucher on the table before Dor Lassos. The Kid, who had obviously come prepared, did the same, adding a thick pile of cash from his gambling of recent weeks.

"That's all of it?" asked Clay.

"All of it," said the Kid.

Clay nodded and stepped back.

"Go ahead," he said.

The Kid turned toward the alien.

"Dor Lassos," he said. "We appreciate your cooperation in this matter."

"I am glad to hear it," responded the Hixabrod, "since my cooperation will cost the winner of the bet a thousand credits."

The abrupt injection of this commercial note threw the Kid momentarily off stride. I, alone in the room, who knew the Hixabrod people, had expected it. But the rest had not, and it struck a sour note, which reflected back on the Kid. Up until now, the bet had seemed to most of the others like a cruel but at least honest game, concerning ourselves only. Suddenly it had become a little like hiring a paid bully to beat up a station-mate.

But it was too late now to stop; the bet had been made. Nevertheless, there were murmurs from different parts of the room.

The Kid hurried on, fearful of an interruption. Clay's savings were on his mind.

"You were a member of the mapping survey team?" he asked Dor Lassos.

"I was," said the Hixabrod.

"Then you know the planet?"

"I do."

"You know its geography?" insisted the Kid.

"I do not repeat myself." The eyes of the Hixabrod were chill and withdrawn, almost a little baleful, as they met those of the Kid.

"What kind of a planet is it?" The Kid licked his lips. He was beginning to recover his usual self-assurance. "Is it a large planet?"

"No."

"Is Tarsus a rich planet?"

"No."

"Is it a pretty planet?"

"I did not find it so."

"*Get to the point!*" snapped Clay with strained harshness.

The Kid glanced at him, savoring this moment. He turned back to the Hixabrod.

"Very well, Dor Lassos," he said, "we get to the meat of the matter. Have you ever heard of Lulungomeena?"

"Yes."

"Have you ever been to Lulungomeena?"

"I have."

"And do you truthfully—" for the first time, a fierce and burning anger flashed momentarily in the eyes of the Hixabrod; the insult the Kid had just unthinkingly given Dor Lassos was a deadly one—"*truthfully* say that in your considered opinion Lulungomeena is the most wonderful place in the Universe?"

Dor Lasso turned his gaze away from him and let it wander over the rest of the room. Now, at last, his contempt for all there was plain to be read on his face.

"*Yes, it is,*" said Dor Lassos.

He rose to his feet at the head of the stunned group around the table. From the pile of cash he extracted a thousand credits, then passed the remainder, along with the two account books and the vouchers, to Clay. Then he took one step toward the Kid.

He halted before him and offered his hands to the man—palms up, the tips of his fingers a scant couple of inches short of the Kid's face.

"My hands are clean," he said.

His fingers arced; and, suddenly, as we watched, stubby, gleaming claws shot smoothly from those fingertips to tremble lightly against the skin of the Kid's face.

153

"Do you doubt the truthfulness of a Hixabrod?" his robot voice asked.

The Kid's face was white and his cheeks hollowed in fear. The needle points of the claws were very close to his eyes. He swallowed once.

"No—" he whispered.

The claws retracted. The hands returned to their owner's sides. Once more completely withdrawn and impersonal, Dor Lassos turned and bowed to us all.

"My appreciation of your courtesy," he said, the metallic tones of his voice loud in the silence.

Then he turned and, marching like a metronome, disappeared through the doorway of the recreation room and off in the direction of his quarters.

"And so we part," said Clay Harbank as we shook hands. "I hope you find the Dorsai Planets as welcome as I intend to find Lulungomeena."

I grumbled a little. "That was plain damn foolishness. You didn't have to buy me out as well."

"There were more than enough credits for the both of us," said Clay.

It was a month after the bet and the two of us were standing in the Deneb One spaceport. For miles in every direction, the great echoing building of this central terminal stretched around us. In ten minutes I was due to board my ship for the Dorsai Planets. Clay himself still had several days to wait before one of the infrequent ships to Tarsus would be ready to leave.

"The bet itself was damn foolishness," I went on, determined to find something to complain about. We Dorsai do not enjoy these moments of emotion. But a Dorsai is a Dorsai. I am not apologizing.

"No foolishness," said Clay. For a moment a shadow crossed his face. "You forget that a real gambler bets only on a sure thing. When I looked into the Hixabrod's eyes, I was sure."

"How can you say 'a sure thing?' "

"The Hixabrod loved his home," Clay said.

I stared at him, astounded. "But you weren't betting on Hixa. Of course he would prefer Hixa to any other place in the Universe. But you were betting on Tarsus—on Lulungomeena—remember?"

The shadow was back for a moment on Clay's face. "The bet was certain. I feel a little guilty about the Kid, but I warned him that gambling money never stuck. Besides, he's young and I'm getting old. I couldn't afford to lose."

"Will you come down out of the clouds," I demanded, "and explain this thing? Why was the bet certain? What was the trick, if there was one?"

"The trick?" repeated Clay. He smiled at me. "The trick was that the Hixabrod could not be otherwise than truthful. It was all in the name of my birthplace—Lulungomeena."

He looked at my puzzled face and put a hand on my shoulder.

"You see, Mort," he said quietly, "it was the name that fooled everybody. Lulungomeena stands for something in my language. But not for any city or town or village. Everybody on Tarsus has his own Lulungomeena. Everybody in the Universe has."

"How do you figure that, Clay?"

"It's a word," he explained. "A word in the Tarsusian language. It means 'home.' "

Time Grabber

Feb. 16, 2631—Dear Diary: Do I dare do it? It's so frustrating to have to be dependent upon the whims of a physicist like Croton Myers. I'm sure the man is a sadist—to say nothing of being a pompous ass with his scientific double-talk, and selfish to boot. Otherwise, why won't he let me use the time-grapple? All that folderol about disrupting the fabric of time.

He actually patted me on the shoulder today when I swallowed my righteous indignation to the extent of pleading once more with him. "Don't take it so hard, Bugsy," he said—imagine— 'Bugsy'—to me, Philton J. Bugsomer, B.A., M.A., L.L.D., Ph.D., "in about twenty years it'll be out of the experimental stage. Then we'll see if something can't be done for you."

It's intolerable. As if a little handful of people would be missed out of the whole Roman Empire. Well, if I can't do it with his permission, I will do it without. See if I don't. My reputation as a scholar of sociomatics is at stake.

Feb. 18, 65: MEMO TO CAPTAIN OF THE POLICE: The emperor has expressed a wish for a battle between a handful of gladiators and an equal number of Christians. Have gladiators but am fresh out of Christians. Can you help me out?

(signed) Lictus,
CAPTAIN OF THE ARENA

Feb. 19, 65: MEMO TO CAPTAIN OF THE ARENA: I think I might be able to lay my hands on a few Christians for you—possibly. And then again I might not. By the way, that's a nice little villa you have out in the Falernian Hills.

(signed) Papirius,
CAPTAIN OF POLICE

Feb. 19, 65: Papirius:

All right, you robber. The villa's yours. But hurry! We've only got a few days left.

L.

Feb. 21, 65: Dear L:

Thanks for the villa. The papers just arrived. By an odd coincidence I had overlooked the fact that we already had sixteen fine, healthy Christians on hand, here. I am sending them on to you.

Love and kisses,
P.

Feb. 22, 2631: Dear Diary: Congratulate me! I knew my chance would come. Late last night I sneaked into the physics building. That fool of a Myers hadn't even had the sense to lock the door of his laboratory. I opened it and went in, pulled down the shade, turned on the light, and was able to work in complete security. Luckily, I had already played on his credulity to the extent of representing myself as overawed by the mechanical mind, and so induced him to give me a rough idea of how he operated the time-grapple (this over the lunch table in the Faculty Club) so, with a little experimenting, and—I will admit it—some luck, I was able to carry off my plans without a hitch.

I bagged sixteen young males from the period of Nero's reign—along somewhere in the last years. By great good luck they happened to be Christians taken prisoner and destined for the Roman Games. Consequently the guards had them all huddled together in a tiny cell. That's why the time-grapple was able to pick up so many at one grab. They came along quite docilely, and I have quartered them in the basement of my house where they seem to be quite comfortable and I can study them at my leisure.

Wait until the Sociomatics department here at the University sees the paper I'll write on this!

Feb. 23, 65: MEMO TO CAPTAIN OF POLICE: Where are my Christians? Don't you think you can gyp me out of my villa and then not deliver.

(signed) Lictus,
CAPTAIN OF ARENA

Feb. 23, 65: MEMO TO CAPTAIN OF THE ARENA: You got your Christians. I saw them delivered myself. Third cell on the right, beneath the stands.

(signed) Papirius,
CAPTAIN OF POLICE

Feb. 24, 65: MEMO TO CAPTAIN OF POLICE: I tell you they're not there.

(signed) Lictus,
CAPTAIN OF THE ARENA

Feb. 24, 65: MEMO TO CAPTAIN OF ARENA: And I tell you they are:

(signed) Papirius,
CAPTAIN OF POLICE

P.S. Are you calling me a liar?

Feb. 25, 65: MEMO TO CAPTAIN OF POLICE: I tell you THEY'RE NOT THERE. Come on over and look for yourself if you don't believe me.

(signed) Lictus,
CAPTAIN OF THE ARENA

Feb. 25, 65: Listen, Lictus:

I don't know what kind of a game you think you're playing, but I haven't time to bother with it right now.

Whether you know it or not, the Games load a lot of extra work on the police. I'm up to my ears in details connected with them, and I won't put up with having you on my neck, too. I've got the receipt signed by your jailer, on delivery. Any more noise from your direction and I'll turn it, together with your recent memos, over to the Emperor himself and you can straighten it out with him.

Papirius

Feb. 25, 2631: Dear Diary: What shall I do? How like that sneaky, underhanded physicist to be studying historical force lines in the Roman era, without mentioning it to me. Myers came into lunch today fairly frothing with what can only be described as childish excitement and alarm. It seems he had discovered a hole in the time fabric in the year 65, although he hasn't so far been able to place its exact time and location (this is, of course, my sixteen Christians) and he tried to frighten us all with lurid talk about a possible time collapse or distortion that might well end the human race—if the hole was not found and plugged. This is, of course, the most utter nonsense. Time collapse, indeed! But I can take no chances on his discovering what actually happened, and so I realized right away that I had to plug the hole.

The idea of putting back my Romans is, of course, unthinkable. They are beginning to respond in a most interesting manner to some spatial relationship tests I have been giving them. Therefore I cleverly sounded out Myers to find the necessary factors to plug the hole. I gather that any sixteen men would do, provided they conformed to the historically important characteristics of the Roman group. This sounded simple when he first said it, but since then the problem has been growing in my mind. For the important characteristics are clearly that they be all Christians who are willing to die for their faith. I might easily find such a group in Roman times but in order to hide the gap my replacements will make I will have to take them from some other era—one Myers is not studying. I have only a day or two at most. Oh, dear diary, what shall I do?

PHYSICIST GIVEN KNOCKOUT
DROPS

(*University News*)

(Feb. 27, 2631). When Croton Myers, outstanding physicist and professor of Physical Sciences at the university here showed a marked tendency to snore during his after-lunch classes, his students became alarmed and carried him over to the University Hospital. There, doctors discovered that the good professor had somehow been doped. There were no ill effects, however, and Dr. Myers was awake and on his feet some eighteen hours later. Authorities are investigating.

Feb. 29, 2631: Dear Diary: SUCCESS! Everything has been taken care of. I am so relieved.

Feb. 28, 1649 (From the Journal of John Stowe)—Today, by the will of the Lord, we are safely on our way from Appleby, fifteen men under the valiant leadership of Sergeant Flail-of-the-Lord Smith, having by our very presence in Appleby served to strike fear into the hearts of the papist plotters there, so that they dispersed—all of the troop in good health and spirits save only for one small trouble, of which I will relate.

It hath come to pass, that, being on our way from Appleby to Carlisle, there to join the forces of Captain Houghton, if God shall suffer such to come to pass, we have found ourselves at nightfall in a desolate section of the country, wasted by the late harrying and pillaging. We decided to pitch camp where we found ourselves rather than adventure farther in the dark.

Therefore, we made ourselves comfortable with such simple fare as contents a servant of the Lord, and our provisions supplied, and having sung a goodly hymn and given ourselves over to an hour or so of prayer for the pleasing of our souls, some among us fell to talking of the nature of the surrounding waste, recalling that from heathen times it hath had the name of being a place of most evil and supernatural resort. But our good Sergeant Flail-of-

161

the-Lord, speaking up cheerily, rebuked those who talked so, saying "Are we not all servants of the Lord, and strong in his wrath? Therefore, gird ye up your courage and take heart."

But there were still some among us—and I do confess some sort of the same weakness in myself—who found the blackness and desolation press still heavily upon our souls, reminding us of manifold sins and wickedness whereby we had placed ourselves in danger of the Pit and the ever-present attacks of the Enemy. And our good Sergeant, seeing this, and perceiving we needed the sweet comfort and assuagement of the Word of the Lord, he bade us sit close by him, and opening his Book which was the Word of the Lord, read to us from II Kings Chapter 9, concerning the overthrow and just fate of Jezebel, whereat we were all greatly cheered and entreated him that he read more to us.

But it happened at this time that a small trouble was thrust upon us, inasmuch as it appeared to all of us that the wide and empty fields of night which surrounded us were whisked away and the appearance of a cell, stone on three sides, and a thick iron grating on the fourth, surrounded us. Whereat we were at first somewhat surprised. However, our good Sergeant, looking up from his Book, bade us mind it not, for that it was no more than a manifestation of whatever unholy spirits plagued the spot and which they had called up in jealous defiance of the sweet virtue of the Lord's word, as he had been reading it.

On hearing this, all were reassured, and, the hour being late, lay down to rest, inasmuch as we are to march at the first break of dawn. So, now, as I write these words, by God's mercy, nearly all are disposed to slumber, saving that the enchantment of the cell doth make somewhat for cramped quarters and I do confess that I, myself, am somewhat ill-at-ease, being accustomed to the good pressure of my stout sword against my side as I go to sleep. This, however, may not be helped, for, since it is the custom of our troop to lay aside all sharp tools on coming into the presence of the Lord our weapons are hidden from